THE OTHER MRS EDEN

BECKY ALEXANDER

Storm

Permission to quote from *Mosquitoes* by Lucy Kirkwood, granted by Nick Hern Books.
www.nickhernbooks.co.uk

Shakespeare quote in the epigraph is from *Henry VI, Part 1*

To request permissions, contact the publisher at rights@stormpublishing.co

Ebook ISBN: 978-1-80508-369-6
Paperback ISBN: 978-1-80508-371-9

Cover design: Emma Graves
Cover images: Shutterstock

Published by Storm Publishing.
For further information, visit:
www.stormpublishing.co

ALSO BY BECKY ALEXANDER

Someone Like You

For everyone waiting in the wings

'When envy breeds unkind division:
there comes the ruin.'

W. Shakespeare

ACT 1

ONE

KIM

'She's a total bitch. Good luck.'

I watched the woman march down the path towards the road, banging the gate behind her. What a welcome to No 1 Clifton Villas. I stared up at the house. White, immaculate and huge. Wide, stone steps, leading to a black door, framed on both sides by expensive-looking potted trees. The house must be, what, four storeys, or five? Did they own the whole place? Where I lived, this would have been broken up into six homes, maybe more. *Just how rich are these people?*

I should have listened to the woman's warning, and left there and then. Life might have turned out very differently. But back then, I didn't have a whole lot of options available to me. So, I took a deep breath and knocked on the door.

'You're late. The agency said you'd be here at ten. I expect punctuality.'

'Sorry. The bus left me at the bottom of the hill... It took longer to walk here than I expected.'

'Well, now you know. Be on time.'

I nodded.

'Your first job will be to hire a new cleaner. The last one left just a few minutes ago. She was useless anyway. I'm sure she was helping herself to my perfume. I could smell it on her. So weird.'

Jemima Eden. I hadn't expected her to open the door herself – maybe something about the expensive house made me expect a butler of some kind. *Get a grip, Kim, this isn't* Downton Abbey. She looked exactly like she did in her films. Tall, thin, flawless skin, and that famous, long red hair. All the photos of her online seemed to be at glamorous red-carpet events, in amazing couture dresses, so it was a little unsettling to see Jemima Eden in grey sweatpants and a T-shirt. She almost looked normal. But, of course, she wasn't. I was beginning to regret my tailored black trousers and white blouse – I had tried too hard and got it wrong. I looked like a waiter.

'Follow me.'

I did as I was told, and left the cavernous hallway, past the staircase, and into the largest, and most stylish kitchen I had ever seen, in real life or on TV. We moved toward a kitchen island, placed perfectly between two enormous sash windows. Did anyone ever cook in here? It looked so tidy.

'Sit.' Jemima indicated a stool, and I perched a little awkwardly, watching as she made herself an espresso from a machine that wouldn't have looked out of place in a coffee shop. She didn't offer me one.

'I hope you're better than the last girl the agency sent. Hopeless. And, really, this is a dream job for the right person. Are you that person?' Jemima glanced at a pile of papers on the granite worktop. I spotted my CV, among others. '...Kim?'

At least she had my name right.

'Yes, and thank you so much for this opportunity.' I smiled, using my best acting skills to show her that yes, I was delighted to be here, and all my life I had wanted to work as a temporary personal assistant for a spoilt, rich actress. She seemed convinced and nodded.

'The hours are irregular. I might need you at any time. It isn't a nine-to-five job, so if that's what you are looking for, then you can leave now.'

The agency had warned me about the hours, but beggars can't be choosers. I didn't have any admin experience, wasn't great on a computer, and, well, to be fair, hadn't really even had a proper job before... well, not much that I could put on a CV, anyway. Jemima Eden didn't need to know how I'd paid my rent for the past few months. Looking at her, I didn't think she would understand.

'You'll need this.' Jemima slid an iPhone across the kitchen counter to me. 'All the contact details you will need are in there. My calendar is on it. You'll need to book my appointments for me, answer calls. Deal with annoying emails that come in – fan mail, requests for interviews, that sort of thing. Book my driver. Book restaurants. Tickets. Run errands. Help my life run smoothly, basically. My agent knows to call me directly about anything very important, so you can handle pretty much everything else that comes in. You'll learn as we go. We can use today as a trial day.'

Great, so the job wasn't actually yet mine. I would need to be on my best behaviour today.

Jemima took a sip from her tiny coffee cup and looked at me carefully. 'You'll need to dress appropriately if you are representing me. Do you have other clothes?' I thought of my small wardrobe at home – jeans, leggings, a couple of charity shop dresses. Nothing that would look right in this house.

'There are bags of my old clothes in the basement that need to go to charity. That can be one of your first tasks – get rid of those. But maybe look through and see if there is anything that fits you.' She looked at me, scanning up and down. 'Maybe some of the more forgiving garments will work... with some adjustments.'

'Thanks, that's really kind of you.'

She beamed at me. 'Great! OK, I think we can make this work. I'll show you around.'

And just like that, I started working for Jemima Eden. Yes, *that* Jemima Eden. The one you will have seen on TV, in movies, on Instagram. Though, thinking about it, I hadn't seen her in anything for a while. But maybe she was so rich she didn't have to work that often.

She was smaller in real life, as they sometimes say about actors, more delicate-looking. Though there was nothing delicate about her, really. She had made that clear already.

I wonder... why is it some people become famous, and some don't?

I'd desperately wanted to be an actor, but it hadn't worked out. I mean, in many ways, we actually looked very similar. I was the same height as Jemima Eden, similar build, similar face in some ways. Yet here I was, two years after leaving school, broke and a failure. The best I could do was temp for someone else, to work to make someone else's life better, smoother. Because my own life had stalled before it even got started. And here she was, in this incredible house, successful, with everything she ever wanted.

I followed Jemima out into the hallway, and the tour began. The ground floor comprised the hallway, kitchen and an ornate dining room on the left, with a vast chandelier hanging over a table that could easily seat twenty. On the right of the hallway was a living room so large the two comfy sofas looked small in the space. An actual grand piano! The walls were lined with books and paintings, though it didn't look very lived-in, as if no one ever relaxed on those sofas. There was no sign of children, or pets, or any sign of everyday life, no cups left lying around, or magazines being read.

I tried to imagine myself living here, with my own furniture, my own taste. It was a dream house, like the house in *Mary Poppins*. High ceilings, big windows, beautiful views out to the street, but above it all, looking down on the people who passed by.

I followed her along a corridor. 'My office,' Jemima indicated with a flourish, another vast room, with a balcony overlooking the beautiful garden below. A large, antique desk with an open laptop, and piled with papers – scripts, by the look of it. Modern artworks lined the walls, giving it the feel of an expensive member's club. On the far wall, a sleek, glass cabinet, filled with shiny awards. I stepped closer, eager to take a good look. Inside, behind the awards, framed black-and-white photos, some signed – Jemima with famous actors, at parties. One of her in her most famous role, in that Bond film. A framed page of script, annotated. Wow. The career she had, I could only dream of.

'Never touch that.'

I could sense Jemima right behind me, smell her perfume, something rich, overpowering.

'Sorry. I meant... are all those awards yours?' I managed, stepping away from the cabinet.

'Yes. George keeps his in his own office. You don't need to go in there.'

'George?' I acted like I didn't know who George Eden was, even though I'd read everything about them both on Wikipedia before I'd turned up. George Eden was also an actor, though less well-known than Jemima. He was one of those actors that you've seen in lots of things, but don't quite remember his name. You'd know his face, if I showed you a photo. Never the leading man, always playing the character part, or the bad guy. I was amazed when I read the list of films he'd been in – so many blockbusters. He'd played apes, aliens and gangster sidekicks. I wondered when I would meet him.

'Upstairs is our bedroom, dressing rooms... You might need to go up there if I need something. Help with my wardrobe, that sort of thing.' This place must have loads of bedrooms, but it was just the two of them, right? And to think there are whole families living in one-bedroom flats.

'Let's finish downstairs.' I followed her back down the corridor, and into the kitchen. Tucked away at the far end was a narrow, gloomy staircase.

'You go first.'

I walked down the stairs, with my hand on the wall. It was so narrow, there was barely room for one person, and no room for a banister. At the bottom was a door, older than the ones upstairs, with paint peeling away to reveal the brown wood below.

I pushed open the door into a dark room with low ceilings, a complete contrast to the airy and spacious rooms above. Jemima flicked a switch, and an overhead plastic light spluttered into life, casting a sickly yellow glow around the room. I could see a chair, a table, and an old, saggy sofa, set under a tiny, barred window. Piles of bins bags, shopping bags, and cardboard boxes covered the floor. Selfridges, Harrods, Harvey Nichols... thick cardboard bags with ribbon handles from so many expensive shops. Delivery boxes, opened, and then, what...? She hadn't bothered to return the contents? Was Jemima a hoarder? Or maybe she was just too busy to deal with this stuff.

'It could do with cheering up, but you can use this as an office, if you need to. Leave your coat here, take breaks, make a coffee, that sort of thing.' She had to be joking. It was so cold and damp down here, even though it was summer outside. The message was clear – here is where you stay out of my way, when I don't want you.

I saw Jemima rub her arms, as if to get warm. 'Come on, let's get started.'

. . .

Here was my list of tasks on day one, barked at me as I followed her upstairs:

- *Book hair appointment, urgently*
- *Print out music for today's piano lesson*
- *Set out lunch at one*
- *Collect shoe order from Selfridges*
- *Sort old clothes*
- *Order sushi delivery for tonight*

'Here is our house credit card. Use this when you need to pay for anything. And, Kim? I need to see all receipts.'

Jemima handed me a black card, and then left me standing in the kitchen. How was I going to fit in everything she'd asked me to do? It would take me hours to get to Selfridges and back, but I needed to be here at one to prepare lunch. Surely she could get the shoes delivered? But no. She said to collect today. She must be going out later. OK, save that task for this afternoon, and get the other things out of the way first.

Everything took me longer than it should, not helped by Jemima's printer being ancient and out of ink. Surely with all their money they could afford better than this. I should order them a new one. I looked at the card in my hand. *I could buy anything with this.*

Lunch came round faster than expected, my stomach reminding me that I hadn't eaten much that day myself. I opened the enormous fridge to see rows of plastic boxes, each labelled with the date, protein content, and serving instructions. What was I meant to do? Put it on a plate for her? Couldn't she do this herself? I guessed this was what happened when you became rich and famous – you become incapable of doing even the simplest task.

OK, I'll play the game.

I found a pretty plate and carefully slid the salmon and chopped salad onto it. I placed the wedge of lime on the salmon, just so. I selected a glass, a bottle of Evian, added ice from the door in the fridge, and placed it all in the dining room, at one end of the table. *She can sit there and eat like a queen if she likes.*

I texted her:

> Lunch is served.

One o'clock on the dot. *She'll be pleased with that.*

The sun was streaming in through the sash windows; it was a rare, hot day in London. The journey to Selfridges was going to be a living hell, and I knew I'd feel sweaty in these nylon black trousers.

I could hear her coming down the stairs, so it was time to make myself scarce. Lunch time for me, too, though the cheese sandwich I'd packed this morning had lost its appeal.

I stood in the basement and looked around. I couldn't believe she was serious about me working down here. They had so much space upstairs, they could shut the door on this place, and never use it. The sooner I got rid of the bags of clothes, I wouldn't need to be down here so much. I could take a few bags with me to drop off when I went to get the shoes.

I started to open the bags, carefully, pulling apart the thick black ribbons, gently opening the tissue paper inside, so as not to tear it. So many gorgeous clothes, I couldn't believe it! Many still had the tags on. Did she really not want this stuff? A stunning grey silk dress. A floaty pink blouse, with tiny beads all over it. Ankle boots in velvet green. Flared jeans in the softest denim I had ever felt. *I'd better check with her on this posh stuff, maybe I could return it for her.* It was too good for a charity shop.

I tipped a bin bag out on to the floor. In this bag, just knitwear. So soft, in all colours of the rainbow – real cashmere! There was nothing wrong with any of it. Why was Jemima getting rid of all these clothes? Because she was bored?

Jemima had said to help myself to the clothes I needed for work, but none of this looked like work clothes... at least, not the sort of thing my mum would have ever worn to work. I tipped out another bag. In this one, summer T-shirts, skirts, a dress. Everything was in size 8, so a bit small for me; it was a squeeze, but worth a try. The dress was looser than the other items. Pale blue, short-sleeved, with a full skirt. So beautiful. Not my usual thing at all. But if it fit, it would be cool on a day like today – would she mind? I pulled off my clothes and slipped the dress over my body, the expensive fabric gliding over my skin.

In the corner of the room was a tiny shower room with a stained wash basin. The light didn't work, but if I left the door open, there was just about enough light to function. I could only see my top half in the mirror over the sink, but it clearly fit perfectly. I looked pale in the mirror – I should have put more make-up on this morning, coming to work here. But somehow, the expensive dress made me look a bit better.

I glanced at the pile of clothes on the floor around me. She would have no idea if I took all these back to their shops, or to the charity shop, or not. I could keep a few things, couldn't I? Jemima had even said I could, for work. I ran my fingers over a cream cashmere vest. Or I could sell some of them. Even if I got fired at the end of today, I could get something out of this.

'Kim!'

I looked up, startled.

'I need to show you the security system before you go out,' Jemima yelled down the stairs.

'Yes, Jemima.'

I ran up the stairs to find her standing in the hallway looking impatient. Jemima opened the cupboard by the front door and tapped in the code.

'You need to set this every time you go out. And disable it when you come in. There are cameras outside, and here, in the hallway.'

I looked up to see a tiny camera, blinking away.

'There are different settings for when we are in the house, at night, and when we are out. It is incredibly important that you get this right, do you understand?'

I nodded, trying to take it all in.

'OK, you try. Show me how you set it when you go out.'

My hand shook a little as I pressed the buttons; I really didn't want to set off the alarm, but I remembered the code (it was the date Jemima had bought the house, she told me) and the screen showed 'Alarm set', as it was meant to.

'I'm going to have a nap, but you've got plenty of tasks to get on with, haven't you?'

I nodded.

'You've changed clothes. Good. You do look more... suitable.'

I wasn't sure how to reply to that.

'Don't just stand there. I'll text you if I think of anything else I need.'

Well, that told me. I was glad to get outside, and back into the real world.

TWO

KIM

'So, what's she like? Your new boss?'

Max poured himself a mug of coffee from the pot I had just made. Without asking.

'She's rich. Doesn't seem to have much to do. Never really goes out. Just sends me out to get shopping for her, answer emails, that sort of thing.'

'Posh housewife, that sort of thing? Married to a Russian?'

'Not met the husband yet. He might be.' I knew exactly who Jemima's husband was, but I wasn't going to tell Max anything. He was one of the worst gossips I knew. I still hadn't met George, but I was looking forward to it. Jemima had mentioned that he was due back from a work trip soon, filming in Budapest. The pair of them had such glamorous lives!

Max had left piles of washing up again, pans stacked in the sink, dirty, congealed water brimming over the top. Clothes heaped next to the washing machine; I could see his pants crumpled on top. So disgusting. Mum would have been horrified to see me living here. Our family home had always been pristine. Small, yes, but every room was homely, warm, and welcoming. Dishes washed up after every meal, and put away without fail. Fresh flowers in the vase on the table, cut from her allotment. How much longer would I have to stay in this stinking flat? Max coming in late after his shifts at the club, always waking me up with his music, too wired or stoned to go to sleep. But it was cheap, close to the city centre, and was all I could afford.

There was no way I was telling him I was working for Jemima Eden – I wanted to keep that secret for me, right now. It was very early days still. I had got through week one at least, acting on my best behaviour. I was due there at ten, and needed to get going if I wasn't going to be late. I started to put keys, phone and lunch in my bag.

'Kim... before you go. We need to pay the gas and electricity bills. It's £400. Can you send me your half?'

£400! It was him who used all the hot water and played music late into the night. Jemima wasn't due to pay me until the end of the month. I would need to stall him until then. I could get £200 quickly if I really needed to, but the thought of that made me shudder. I didn't want to have to do that unless I was desperate. Max could wait.

'Sure! Will sort that out later. Got to go.'

'You're late.'

Jemima was standing in the hallway when I arrived, just a few minutes after ten.

'So sorry. The train was really slow today.'

'Leave earlier, then. I can't bear lateness. I told you that on your first day.'

She turned and walked fast towards her office. This wasn't good. I assumed I was meant to follow, and did so, like an obedient puppy.

Jemima threw herself down on a sofa, and indicated for me

to sit opposite. She had a serious look on her face. Was she going to fire me? For being five minutes late?

'I need you to go through my social media and do some replies. Do you think you can manage that? No need to reply to every comment of course, just pick a few, and if they have a blue tick, or you recognise their name, reply with something lovely. Can you do that? I find it so tedious, but it's important to keep your engagement up.'

Oh! Not firing me, then. 'Don't you have an agent who does that sort of thing?' It seemed strange her asking me – what did she want me to reply to them? It was the wrong question to ask. Jemima stared at me.

'Elle and her team don't have time for that. No. This is part of *your* job. Do you have a problem with it?'

I shook my head. If she wanted me to pretend to be her on social media, I could do that.

'Good. I hate that stuff.' Jemima stood up as if to leave, then paused. 'What are you wearing?'

I glanced down. Green floaty trousers and a white T-shirt. I had found them in her bag of cast-offs. Did she want them back? I looked up at her, saw her evaluating me. Had I messed up? She *had* wanted to get rid of these clothes, hadn't she?

'Better. You look less...' And with that, she walked out of the room.

I logged into Jemima's social media feeds and scrolled through her page. She had nearly a million followers! Wow. I had about a hundred. Her last post was a photo of her on holiday in Ibiza, on a clifftop, looking out to sea and a beautiful sunset. It looked like a professional photoshoot. I wondered who had taken it? Her husband, George? It might have been an actual professional for all I knew. Maybe that's what celebrities did. It had been posted yesterday when I knew damn well she had been here all day. Oh, well, that was all part of the game, I guess. Her online followers didn't need to know the truth.

She had hundreds of likes and comments. I scrolled through, reading them. It hardly felt like work, but hey, she was paying me.

> You look amazing!!
>
> Love that dress. Where did you get it?
>
> Great sandals. Where are they from?
>
> Are you filming??? What's next for you!!

And lots of heart emojis. People could be so basic. Did they really think someone like Jemima Eden would reply to them, or care if they posted a heart?

And then, further down:

> That dress does nothing for you. I wouldn't wear it.
>
> TERF! Why don't you say what you really think!!!
>
> Rich bitch.

Oh my god. So many opinions. Jealous, I'm sure, most of them. Or trolls.

I typed in a few 'thanks xx' to the nice comments, and blocked some of the negative ones. No wonder Jemima wanted someone else to do this.

The little arrow in the corner showed that she had lots of direct messages. I clicked on it. And then wished I hadn't. So many nasty photos – of dicks, of porn. This naked pic was of Jemima! This couldn't be her, really could it? Her face stuck on someone else's body, I thought. I deleted it quickly. *Block.* Did she ever look at this stuff? Of course she did... that's why she wanted me to do this for her. Clearly being famous had its downsides, but then, if you had enough money, you could get someone else to deal with this shit, and make it all go away. I was happy to oblige.

We quickly got into a pattern. Being a famous actress seemed a lot like being a bored housewife. I was surprised that Jemima hardly ever went out, but then, she had everything she needed right here in this incredible house. If I lived here, I'd stay in, too.

One morning, just after I'd arrived, a personal trainer came to the house and Jemima did a workout in the garden. She also seemed to do Pilates or yoga or something upstairs most mornings, as I could hear wind chimes and chilled music drifting through the house. A chef arrived with boxes packed with meals, each one perfectly portioned out. A little stack of breakfast pots, and lunch salads, and evening meals. It was my job to reheat them, steam the vegetables, and plate them up before I left each day. I brought my lunch from home or from the supermarket down by the bus stop, and kept it in the basement until I had a break.

Jemima mostly stayed in her bedroom or office, and I let people into the house when needed. One morning, a hair stylist came. She was really nice, so friendly. I offered her a cup of tea to take up with her.

'That's so kind, but I'm good, thanks. Had a matcha latte on the way in. You're new here, right?'

I nodded. Louella introduced herself, and told me she'd been coming here every month for a year. She had the most amazing shiny hair, perfect in every way. My hand went to my own hair – I felt drab in comparison.

'How you getting on?' she asked, putting her jacket in the cloakroom. She clearly knew her way around the place.

'Good, thanks.'

'Hope you last longer than the last one. She was nice, but no match for...' She indicated up the stairs, and gave me a big smile. 'See you later.'

Jemima emerged later that day with perfectly blow-dried hair, but she didn't go out afterwards; she just went into her home office. A weird life, but then, I guess she could hardly pop out to the shops without getting hassled. To be honest, I'd be quite happy, if I had her life. Just pottering around this house, getting my hair done. Lucky bitch.

My work phone pinged.

Office. Now.

Yes, m'lady. It had better not be 'make me a coffee', I thought, as I walked past the kitchen.

Jemima was pacing the room, looking anxious. 'Kim. I need to do a self-tape. Annoying really, as the director knows me. But, anyway... he's in the US, so Elle has asked me to do it. Show willing.'

Elle was her agent. Not sure if I told you that? Jemima was always very happy to take her calls.

Jemima had tied her long red hair back into a high ponytail, and it made her look younger, softer somehow. Behind her, a pale grey screen was lowering from the ceiling. It stopped silently, making a perfect background for filming.

'Do you know what a self-tape is?' she asked me. I nodded. I'd done a few, trying to get into drama school.

'Great. OK, I need you to read the lines of the other part. Just quietly, of course. They don't need to hear you. Just me. You stand there. That's it. I will stand here.' I watched her position herself in front of the screen, clip on a tiny microphone, and look at the camera. It looked like a professional camera. No iPhone self-tape for her.

'Oh god, the lighting is terrible. Too sunny. Hang on.'

Jemima pulled down the blind behind her, darkening the room. 'OK, ready. The script is on the table.'

I picked it up. Stamped across the front page, in black, bold letters it read:

PROPERTY OF NETFLIX. DO NOT SHARE.
SCRIPT 1/8.

'Read from the start, page three. I've highlighted my lines. You read the other parts.' Jemima shook her shoulders, and took a deep breath in, followed by a slow exhale. 'OK, ready.'

Was I really doing this? Reading a script with actual Jemima Eden? I turned to page three, and saw that she had highlighted the part she was playing in neon pink. I took a breath in, trying to be calm, hoped that my voice wouldn't waver, would sound clear, that I would get this right. I used to be good at this.

'Why did you come here? You know it isn't safe.' My first line, done. I glanced up.

'I had to see you.' Jemima said, a little too loudly, in my opinion.

'If he sees us...' I replied.

'We have to find a way forward. For the families to meet. This war between us has gone on for too long.'

What was this? Some sort of fantasy, sci-fi thing? Or maybe something more like *Peaky Blinders*, a gangster show. Filming in the US, Jemima had said.

'Kim! That was your line. For god's sake. We'll have to start again. Idiot. All you have to do is *read*. Pay attention.' She pressed buttons on the camera, deleting the now useless footage. She walked back to her spot in front of the screen.

'Don't mess it up again.'

We made it through to the end of the scene. I realised I had been holding tension in my shoulders, and tried to relax. It was the closest I had been to proper acting in a long time.

'Again.'

We did three more takes, each one slightly different than before. Jemima didn't seem able to get the lines exactly right. By the end of the morning, I felt I knew the script better than her. It wasn't exactly difficult.

'I need a break. Get me a green shot from the kitchen, and then we can go again. Don't mess it up again.'

Me? It was *her* that had messed up, not getting the lines right. When I was at school, I was really good at line-learning. It just went in, made sense to me.

I walked to the kitchen to fetch her vitamin boost thing, doing as I was told. As I poured the green juice into a pretty blue glass, I found myself smiling. How funny. Here she was, the famous actor, and she was finding it hard to learn her lines. Was she *nervous*? How unexpected.

'Here you are. Kale and cucumber.' I held out the juice to Jemima.

I relived what happened next countless times that night. Somehow, as Jemima reached for the glass, it flew out of my hand, shattering and sending thick, green sludge across the floor. We both stood there staring as it spread across the antique rug. How could there be so much of it? Jemima fell to her knees, reaching for the pieces of glass, not noticing that she was leaning in the mess.

'You idiot! Get out! Get out of my sight!'

It took a while for my heart rate to calm down. She had *screamed* at me. It wasn't even my fault – her hand was shaky – she dropped it, not me. Should I go back up there and apologise? Clean up the mess? Yes, I should do that, but she was probably going to fire me anyway, so what was the point? She'd only shout at me again.

I looked around the basement. Even in the middle of a sunny day, it felt cold and damp. I shivered.

Would she come down here to fire me? Or wait until I went upstairs again? Better to face the music than wait down here like some scolded child. I was sure that, in about five minutes, I would be fired, and out of this house forever.

Jemima wasn't in her office.

'Jemima?' I called out, quietly. Had she gone out? More likely she had gone to lie down, which she seemed to do a lot.

I found a roll of kitchen paper and got onto my hands and knees, to try and clean up as much of the green juice as I could. Maybe then she would give me a decent reference, or at least not complain about me to the agency. It felt like the least I could do. I heard footsteps behind me.

'What have we here? A real-life Cinderella?'

I turned, looked up and saw him. George Eden. His voice had that clipped, cut-glass, haughty tone, that only men who have been educated at the most expensive private schools can manage. I'd met a few men like him before – they were very different from the blokes I'd grown up with.

I stood up. 'Hi, I'm Kim. Jemima's PA. Or... I was until I did this. She's probably going to fire me now.'

Leaning against the door frame, George Eden looked at me with a half-smile on his face. He was better-looking than I'd expected. Had a cheerful, relaxed look about him, as if he'd just got back from holiday. Thick, dark hair. His sleeves were rolled up, showing tanned arms. I found myself smiling back at him.

'Oh, Jemima's bark is far worse than her bite. Can I give you a hand?'

We both looked at the mess on the floor. I had managed to mop up the worst of the sludge, but the rug would need to be finished by a specialist cleaner.

'I'm OK, thanks.'

'It's no trouble.' George kneeled next to me and picked up a tiny shard of glass that I'd missed. His arm brushed against mine, as we both stood up. 'Don't worry about this. Everything can be cleaned up.'

He had such a kind face. 'So, how are you getting on? Jem told me about you. She got you running around, doing her shopping?'

I nodded, and smiled back at him.

'A bit of shopping, yes. Answering emails. The phone, if she doesn't want to take the call. Making appointments. A lot of social media.'

'Ah, important work! Well done, you. Sounds like business as usual here, then. Now, I really need a strong coffee. I had a very early flight this morning. Would you like one? Sounds like you've had a rough morning, too.'

I found myself walking towards the kitchen, George's hand on my shoulder. He was clearly used to taking control of a situation.

'What would you like? I'm having a macchiato – want the same?' I had no idea what that was, but nodded.

George worked the coffee machine like a professional barista, then presented me with a tiny cup of coffee, creamy on top. 'It's Blue Mountain. The best coffee in the world. I hope you like it.'

He watched me take a sip. It was so delicious. George leaned on the counter and looked at me, his eyes warm and inquisitive.

'So, what brings you here? Always wanted to work for an actress?'

He seemed genuinely interested in me, which was so kind. Jemima hadn't mentioned he was due back today. Strange that he hadn't gone upstairs to find her yet.

'Actually... I would have loved to be an actor. I tried for

drama school, but... well, it's been hard finding work. So, when this came up, I took it.'

George looked surprised. 'A budding actress! My goodness. Does Jemima know?'

I shook my head.

'I remember starting out. It's so hard!' He sounded so sympathetic. I wondered if he had ever actually struggled to get acting work. It seemed unlikely.

I nodded. 'It is. Sort of soul-destroying really. I did try really hard. I think, maybe, I look too... that my look isn't what they wanted.' I knew that no one would ever describe me as beautiful. Unusual, yes, maybe, with my very pale skin. Or maybe I simply wasn't talented enough.

'Unconventional looks can be an asset. Don't be so hard on yourself. No one would describe me as good-looking – I'm a character actor, through and through,' George said, grinning.

I studied him. His facial features were uneven, I guess, not conventionally handsome, but there was something about him... a confidence that made me want to look at him longer. He held my gaze and I looked away, quickly.

'Right!' He finished his coffee and placed the cup in the dishwasher. Jemima never did that – she left things out all the time for me to put away. 'I'm off to see my beloved.'

He walked briskly to the door, and then paused, looking back at me. 'Are you OK with all the security? Jemima's last PA found it all a bit much.'

'The alarm? Yes, fine, thanks.'

George nodded. 'Good. We have to be so careful here. Let me know if you are worried about any of it. It's very straightforward really.'

He ran his hand through his hair. 'And that thing with the broken glass. Don't worry about it. I'll deal with Jemima. I'm so glad you're here, Kim. Let me know if you ever need anything.'

. . .

I kept busy for the rest of the afternoon, until my shift was over. As I walked up the stairs, my coat and bag in my hand, I wondered if I'd get a message from the agency, firing me. Would I ever be in a house like this again? It seemed so far removed from my life, or anyone I had ever known. And I'd blown it.

I heard Jemima before I saw her.

'Kim!'

'Here. Sorry, Jemima.' I rushed into the hallway to find her standing there, by the front door.

'This isn't working out. I'll pay you for the days you've done, of course. Make sure you have all your stuff, and leave...'

'Now, Jemima, don't be so hasty.' George appeared behind me.

I watched Jemima smooth down her sleeves, try to regain her composure.

'Seems I walked into a drama!' he said.

'I've had a hell of a day. I had to do a self-tape. Me! Elle doesn't seem to have the influence she used to, you know? I should probably be talking to new agents, but instead I'm dealing with all this.'

At that, she waved her thin arm towards me.

'Come on, darling. Elle is so well-known in the industry. No need to overreact.' George was clearly used to this sort of outburst.

'And Kim... she's ruined our rug. And broke the glass my brother gave me. I need someone I can rely on.'

'I'm so sorry. I tried to clean it up.' My heart was beating fast.

'Darling, you are running out of people willing to do your bidding. It was clearly an accident. Why don't you give the poor kid another chance?'

I looked from George to Jemima. George raised his

eyebrows at me.

'I'm really sorry, Jemima. The glass just slipped... I can get the rug cleaned professionally. I'll pay for it. If you want me to stay, I promise it won't happen again. I really do need this job.'

Jemima stared at George, clearly deciding what to say with me standing there. I tried to look contrite. She let out a long exhale.

'OK. One more week. I do have a lot to do. And it is a bloody nightmare trying to find an assistant. Last chance, Kim, OK? And don't smirk, George. It really doesn't suit you.'

'Thanks. It won't happen again.'

Like a miracle, the phone rang in the office and I ran to get it, pleased to get away from the tense atmosphere.

'It's Elle for you, Ms Eden.'

'At last! I've left, what, two messages?'

She snatched the phone out of my hand and stood there, beaming at us both.

I hear a muffled voice at the other end, animated, positive. And then watched as Jemima's face fell, and she turned her back towards us.

George and I just stood there, transfixed.

'Right. OK. Thanks, Elle. It wasn't right for me anyway. Yes, talk soon.'

And then she threw the phone across the room.

THREE

KIM

The last thing I needed when I got in, after the day I'd had, was a house full of Max's obnoxious friends.

'Kim! Haven't seen you for ages.' Letchy Simon pulled me into an awkward hug. I tried not to inhale the stink of beer on his breath.

I pulled away from him. 'Where's Max?' I glanced around, trying to spot him through the crowd. The music was so loud – the family below must hate us. Bottles of real Champagne in the sink, designer beers... If Max could afford all this, why the hell was he pressurising me to pay the stupid bills?

'Wasn't she the one who...' I turned to see two girls who were always hanging around Max. They stopped talking abruptly. Had they been talking about *me*? The shorter one looked away, sheepishly. She had no right to judge me. People like them had no idea. Their parents paid for everything they needed, university fees, a place to live, money to eat. Mum had helped me as much as she could, but I couldn't ask for more. So what if I had done what I had to do? I pushed past the two girls, trying to get to my bedroom. There must have been ten people in the hallway. Max was nowhere to be seen. Dickhead.

I felt exhausted from tip-toeing around Jemima all day, doing her bidding. I really wanted to just crawl into bed and crash out. It would be impossible to sleep with all this noise. Maybe I still had some of Mum's sleeping pills somewhere...

A couple were leaning against the door to my room.

''Scuse me.' They made no attempt to move, lost in the music and their own little world.

'Hello? That's my room!' I tried to make myself heard over the music.

The man noticed me, at last. 'OK, babe. Chill out.'

I pushed my way past them and switched on the light. In my bed, two bodies writhed, underneath *my* duvet. Piles of strangers' clothes were on the floor, *my* floor. A face I didn't recognise, yelling at me. 'Go away, you pervert!'

I turned and pushed my way through the crowd in the corridor and found myself outside in the stairwell, more people coming upstairs, joining the party. How dare Max do this to me? Let people into my room. I wanted to go back in there, get my stuff, and run. But where would I go? I felt tears welling up as I stood there, leaning against the cold, concrete wall, trying to work out what to do.

'You're here nice and early. Good. We have a lot to do this week. I'm throwing a party on Friday. We need to get organised!'

It was a surprise to see Jemima in the kitchen this early. If she was going to make a habit of this, I'd have to be more careful. She hadn't heard me coming up from the basement, had she? No, she would have said...

I'd felt really anxious when I let myself in late last night – would I remember the alarm code, or get it wrong and wake them all up? My heart had thudded as I typed in the code, but it was fine. All was quiet as I walked across the hallway and down into the basement.

I made the sofa as comfy as I could, using one of Jemima's reject coats as a blanket, but I could still feel the damp in the atmosphere. The water in the shower ran cold, but I was at least vaguely clean, dressed, and ready for work before Jemima appeared. I let my shoulders relax. She clearly had no idea I'd stayed overnight.

'Get a notepad, Kim. We need to book caterers. DJ. Flowers. Guest list, of course! A party is exactly what I need. Cheer the place up a bit.'

Jemima reached into the fridge and pulled out a yogurt pot. I'd tried one the other day – it tasted weird. And when I'd read the label I discovered it was some sort of soy product, devoid of any fat and creaminess. I watched her spoon it mechanically into her perfectly shaped mouth.

'Cocktails, and a decent wine list, Kim. Let's get a bartender who can make something delicious when people arrive. Martinis! And do you have a supplier? We need something to perk up the party when it gets late.'

'A... supplier?'

'Yes, you know... pay attention, Kim!'

Was she talking about drugs? Did that also come under my job description? I had no idea how to do that, though I knew Max would. Even if I'd been tempted to try drugs, I'd never had the spare money. Or liked the idea of losing control. Was she serious?

'And I'll need something new to wear. Something gorgeous, to lift my spirits. Maybe we could have the martinis out in the garden if the weather holds. Call The Boutique and ask them to send over some dresses. They know what I like.'

'Yes, Ms Eden.'

'Great!' She smiled, pleased with herself. 'Go on then! Get started.'

. . .

The week was insane. Who knew a dinner party needed so much organising? I hadn't even been to one before, unless you counted sharing a pan of pasta with people from school. And yet here I was, helping to arrange a celebrity dinner. Sixteen people were coming, and they all seemed to have their own special dietary requirements. Jemima shouted at the caterers, who then threatened to pull out on the morning of the party, and I'd had to apologise profusely for her. I was relieved when the chefs started arriving at noon, carrying huge silver containers full of food. Flowers arrived, direct from Cornwall. 'I can't bear hot-house flowers. So tacky. Only get natural flowers,' Jemima had demanded, sending me the link to the grower, who mostly grew plants for Chelsea Flower Show. The flowers had cost almost £700 – more than I was getting paid that week. Mum had grown most of these on her allotment. The idea that some rich woman would pay that much for her flowers would have made her laugh.

'Kim! Where are the dresses? I need to try them on.' Jemima shouted down the stairs.

'I'm waiting for the gardeners to get here, then I'll go and get them.'

That wasn't good enough. I heard her stomp angrily across the landing.

'I need them now! If they aren't right, I need to know. Honestly, Kim. This is the most important thing!'

She had already rejected two dresses that The Boutique had sent over. Three more had been delivered to the shop that morning – new season, early, direct from the designer.

'I'll go now.' *Agree with her. It's the only way.*

'She's such a diva. It's not like she even pays for them.'

The shop assistants could only be talking about one person. Standing there in my grey trousers and T-shirt, I clearly didn't look like someone the two blow-dried lookalikes needed to rush to serve.

'Excuse me. I'm here to pick up the order for Jemima Eden.'

The taller one looked at me, surprised. Embarrassed to be caught out talking about my boss? She looked me up and down, a little too obviously.

'You work for Jemima Eden?' She glanced at her colleague.

'I'm her assistant,' I said, standing a little taller. If they didn't let me take the dresses, Jemima would be furious with me.

'Wait there.' The taller of the two disappeared through a door behind the counter.

The other one stared at me, intrigued. 'How d'you get that job?' she asked, not smiling. Did she want the job for herself, or was she judging me? It was hard to tell.

'Here you go.' The tall assistant appeared with three large cardboard bags. 'Can you make sure she tags the shop in her Insta posts? Return the ones she doesn't wear,' she said, firmly. There is no way she would have spoken to Jemima like that.

'Thank you so much.' There was no mention of payment. I glanced around the shop, at the artfully folded jeans and T-shirts on glass tables, the rails of rainbow-coloured dresses. I never went in places like this – I just knew there was no way I could afford anything.

I felt a bit of a freak sitting on the bus, with the expensive cardboard bags stacked around me. Everyone else had plastic supermarket bags, backpacks, normal stuff. I carefully opened one bag and tried to feel inside the tissue paper wrapping. It felt like silk, so smooth. Embroidered gold threads ran through the fabric, but subtle, too. I could just about reach the tag, attached by its own thin, black ribbon. £1,580. Wow! I pushed it back inside its tissue paper, and held the bags a little closer to me until we arrived at my bus stop.

As I walked up the hill to the house, I could see that everything was happening as planned, with vans parked outside. I followed two men in large padded coats carrying DJ equipment inside. Jemima stood in the hallway, shouting at them to take everything to the garden. I glanced up – clouds were gathering across the bright blue sky. Would the weather hold? The DJ didn't look that happy about it.

'Where have you been? I needed you here,' she barked at me.

'I got the dresses,' I told her as a man walked past, carrying a mini gazebo.

'Take them to my bedroom,' she snapped. *No chance of a thank you, then.*

I have to admit, seeing all the activity in the house as we all prepared for the party was quite cool. It was all so glamorous! I had recognised some of the names on the guest list that I'd invited, and had researched the others online. Jemima clearly knew some really successful people – everyone seemed to be a famous actor, a director or a producer. It was another world. I didn't even have sixteen people I could invite to dinner. I'd never been that great at making friends.

It felt a little weird going into their bedroom, the Edens' intimate space. I'd never been allowed in here before. It was a stunning room, flooded with light from the tall sash windows. There was a pale cream carpet, with a huge bed floating in the centre of the room, piled high with cushions. It smelt of expensive perfume; something musky and citrussy. Large white candles sat on every surface. There was a huge glass chandelier overhead.

To the left, there was a walk-in closet, with shelves lined with neatly folded cashmere sweaters, so soft to the touch. Rows of shoes sat ready for a glamorous night out, most with sharp heels, looking like they'd never been worn. I ran my hand along the rails of dresses – each perfectly aligned on black velvet hangers. I lifted the sleeve of one dress, and let it run through my fingers. I would give anything for a room like this one day.

'Hello there.'

I turned to see George emerge from the shower room, wearing only a towel. Startled, I stepped back, knocking into the bags I had left on the floor beside me.

'I'm... I've got Jemima's dresses for tonight.'

'Have you?' He smiled at me, clearly enjoying that he'd caught me snooping around.

I bent down to pull the first dress out of its bag, to slip it onto a hanger. Was he going to stand there and watch me do this? I felt a blush spread across my face.

'Are you joining us tonight, Kim? It would be nice to have someone there who isn't awful.'

Despite myself, I turned to look at him. 'I'm not invited.'

'Shame. These parties of Jemima's can be very tedious. It would be lovely to have you there. A friendly face. Someone who isn't trying to pitch their new project at me.' He stepped towards me, and then stopped, as if thinking better of it. Still, he was so close I could see the water droplets on his chest.

'Do you need anything?' I asked, awkwardly. I didn't work for him, exactly, but it seemed the polite thing to ask. Keep him onside.

'Me? Oh, I can look after myself. Thank you for asking though. Very sweet of you.'

'I better get downstairs. There's so much to do.' He was standing there, right in my way. *Oh god, if Jemima walked in now, this would look so wrong.*

'See you later, Kim,' he said, and stepped aside. I felt his eyes on me as I scurried out of the room.

FOUR

KIM

It was the perfect evening for a party. Jemima had insisted that we set up the drinks' reception in the garden, and she had been right – the weather had held and it did look amazing out there, with white lights hanging overhead, bobbing in the breeze, the lawn freshly cut and the DJ playing chilled music over in the corner. A small team of gardeners had brought in potted white hydrangeas that morning, and one had spent hours trimming the topiary trees into perfect mounds – it looked like a posh hotel garden. I could see George over by the cherry tree, having a sneaky smoke before the guests arrived. I knew he was on his third drink already, possibly more. Was he nervous? If so, that made two of us. *Just over an hour to go.*

The doorbell rang and I ran to open the door. Three unbelievably good-looking men, all around my age, dressed in smart black suits and white shirts stood there, looking at me, as if expecting me to give them instructions. I had no clue. I looked around, willing the caterer to appear, before it occurred to me that they were probably the servers.

'So, where do you want us, boss?' one said, smiling, showing perfect teeth. He had the most astonishing pale blue eyes.

'Um, you can be here by the door? Take coats? Show people through to the garden when they get here?'

'Sure, no problem.'

Was he an actor? A model? He was too good-looking for this to be his normal job. 'You can put coats there.' I indicated the cloakroom.

'This is some house. Who owns it?' the tallest of the three asked me.

'Jemima and George Eden.'

He whistled. 'Oh wow. The agency said it was a big client.'

I was surprised to find I felt protective of George and Jemima. 'Don't talk to them, or the guests, more than you have to. You can be discreet, right?' I really felt out my depth here, trying to be in charge.

Blue-eyed man shrugged. 'No problem. Got it, boss.' I saw him exchange a glance with the man next to him.

'Hi there. You from the agency?' The caterer, Jan, appeared from the kitchen. 'Follow me. We need help setting up.'

I took one last look around the house. An interiors stylist had come in earlier, and styled the dining table with vintage glassware, fine china plates piled on top of each other, linen napkins, white flowers. I'd taken photos, it looked so magical. It might be good for Jemima's Instagram – I could ask her tomorrow if she wanted this shared. The catering and bar staff all seemed to be getting into place, and a calm, expectant hush had settled in the house. It really was as ready as it could be. I texted Jemima.

> All ready down here. Do you need anything?

A few moments later, her reply appeared.

> Good. Text me when the guests are all here.
> Not a moment before.

I had half an hour before the guests were due to arrive. Right now, I looked far too much like the agency staff – I needed to change, set myself apart. Down to the basement. I had found a black dress in Jemima's reject bags, which I thought would be perfect. Short cap sleeves, fitted top, then flared a little, landing on the knee. It fit me perfectly; I'd lost a little weight since I'd started working here. I wasn't exactly Jemima's size yet, but I wasn't far off. I tied up my hair, leaving a few loose strands to frame my face. It was so hard to get make-up right down here, with this lighting, but I did my best, applying a bit more than usual.

Jemima had been upstairs for hours with Louella. How different to me, down here in this crappy lighting, making do with someone else's cast-offs. I'd seen Louella's invoice. Jemima was paying a lot to look good for a dinner party.

I stared at myself in the mirror. I needed to be bolder, stand out more. Red lipstick would help. I had one, buried in the bottom of my make-up bag, from when I was escorting. I carefully traced my lips, watching them turn from palest pink to a glossy, blood red.

The guests were due to arrive at seven for cocktails, and it was almost time. I felt a surge of adrenaline – the evening felt so full of potential. I might meet some famous people, people with influence. My job was to keep it all running smoothly, to make sure Jemima was happy at all times. How hard could that be? I smoothed down my dress. It almost felt like a theatre performance, the moment before the curtain goes up before a show. If I got this right, it would secure my job here, or might even lead to something better. I was ready.

The doorbell rang.

Two of George's friends were the first to arrive. I told one of the agency staff help to show them through to the garden, where I knew George was hanging out with the DJ.

Next, a chic-looking woman – willowy and Scandinavian-looking, with a shorter, rounder woman next to her.

'Hi. Can I take your name please?'

She stared at me, a small smile forming.

'Elle Lobina. You must be new.'

Jemima's agent. I felt like an idiot.

'I'm so sorry. We've spoken before. I'm the PA.'

She handed me her coat. 'Are they out in the garden?'

I nodded. I hadn't even said my name.

'How many is that now...?' I heard Elle whisper to her companion as they walked past.

More guests arrived, and between me and the blue-eyed agency man, we took coats, showed them through to the garden, arranged parking and generally made people welcome.

'So, do you do a lot of these parties?' I asked him, in a lull between arrivals. 'I'm Kim, by the way. Sorry, I should have said.'

He smiled. 'Damian. Yeah, quite a few. It's easy, flexible. I can fit it in between auditions. I'm an actor.'

I had guessed right.

'Been in anything I would have seen?'

'Not yet, but watch this space,' he replied, grinning.

'Hello! Hope we're not too late!'

I turned to see Rory Jackson, standing in the doorway. Yes, the actual Rory Jackson. Star of so many films, even better looking than on screen. I knew for sure he wasn't on the guest list. I would have known. And next to him, a tiny woman with enormous eyes, and a very sharp fringe. She shrugged off her faux fur coat, revealing a scrap of a dress and impossibly thin legs. Damian couldn't wait to help *her*, stepping right in front of me, blocking my way.

'So, where is she?' Rory asked, glancing up the stairs.

'Jemima?' I said, stupidly. 'Everyone is in the garden. She's nearly ready.'

'Planning her big entrance, I imagine,' he added, winking. 'You must be Kim, the new PA. Rory Jackson.'

He held out his hand, and I shook it, surprised. Jemima had mentioned me? But if he wasn't on the guest list... should I send him away? And we hadn't planned for them at dinner... I was so out of my depth here. But it was Rory Jackson! There was no way I could just tell him to leave. She must have invited him last minute, and not bothered to tell me.

'I'll show you through.'

The pair followed me out to the garden, and I watched as they were greeted by friendly faces and handed martinis by a waiter. The sound of lively conversation mixed with the Balearic beats, as the rich and famous hung out, secure in the knowledge that they truly belonged here, hidden away from the outside world. There was just one person missing. I made the call.

'Jemima. It's time.'

FIVE

JEMIMA

'Darlings! Hello! I am so sorry to keep you all waiting.'

Every face turns towards me as I make my entrance. I know I look incredible. The dress looks even better on than I had hoped, fitting my curves perfectly.

The delicate metallic threads catch the last of the golden hour light, making me sparkle. It does feel slightly chilly on my bare arms and legs, but I was so right to hold the drinks out here – it all looks perfect, and a drink will soon warm me up. Taking in the admiring glances of the people standing below me, I know they will remember this night for a long time.

A ripple of applause breaks out as the guests react to my arrival. I raise my hands in greeting, and I see George walk up the terrace steps.

'Quite the entrance,' he whispers to me.

'Drink, Ms Eden?' A very handsome waiter steps forward with a tray and I select a martini.

Taking a sip, I look around. My guests seem to be having a good time, talking animatedly. I hear Elle before I see her, her loud voice carrying above the music. She needed this reminder of just who exactly I am, the star I am.

I scan around the faces, and there he is. Looking right at me. Our eyes lock, just for a second, and Rory gives me a small, discreet wave. Good, he's shown up. So much for him already having plans. I allow myself a small smile.

Wait... who the hell is that, standing next to him? Cassie someone... I've seen her in something, one of the streaming channels. She has her arm on Rory's. Has he brought a *date*? And she's come dressed like that, to *my* party? I feel irritation rise.

'Come and say hello to Elle,' George says, taking my arm.

We walk slowly down the terrace steps onto the lawn, greeting people as we pass. I see Elle make her way through the crowd towards me.

'Darling!' We air-kiss each other, like best friends. It has been over two weeks since the rejection from Greg and his stupid Netflix film, and I haven't had anything new through from her yet.

'Great party!'

'Thanks! So glad you could fit it into your busy schedule.'

Elle laughed. 'Of course. You're still my number one client, Jemima.'

'It doesn't always feel like that,' I replied. Elle has been with me from the start, and she knows me better than anyone. And I've probably made her more money that anyone.

'You've made it, Jem. Look around. Even people like you get a no, sometimes. It's not the end of the world.'

'So, what are your other clients working on?' A perfectly reasonable question.

'Oh, I can't say too much. You know that.' Elle smiles at me and takes a sip of her drink. 'This is delicious! You always know how to throw a good party.'

I tilt my head at her.

'OK, OK! Daniel has a new film in the pipeline. It might be a little stretch of his acting skills, but you know him, he can charm anyone. But otherwise, things are a little quiet... I'm always talking to people about you, you know that.'

An older man appears next to us, and leans in to kiss me. Some friend of George's, I guess. Well, he can wait his turn. I take Elle's arm. *Not so fast.* I want to have this conversation before the evening gets going.

'I've been thinking, Elle. How about a play for me next? Something here in London? Or a short regional tour around the nice theatres?'

Elle takes a swig of her drink. *Steady old girl, don't want you getting too drunk.*

'Are you still interested in the stage? I thought, after last time... You might want to focus on your TV work, and film. You do shine on the small screen. Some people are doing very well with film voiceovers, too, you know. Well, George can tell you all about that!'

Voiceovers! Me? It's OK for George – he'll do anything if it pays well. But for me, it's about the art. It has been a long time since I was last on a stage, and I miss it. There's something about appearing before an audience that makes you feel so alive.

'I can do it, Elle. Can you look into some options for me?' I notice her glance over my shoulder, and then smile with relief as George appears beside us.

'Elle! Good evening. You look lovely as ever.'

'George, I was just talking to Jemima about voiceover work. It's so much fun, and low stress, of course.'

'I love it! A few days in a studio, that's all. Then let the motion capture experts do all the real hard work. And very good money, of course.' He beams at that, so pleased with himself.

'Not sure that's right for me. I like to be seen by the audience,' I say, then regret it.

I can see the irritation on George's face. We both know he wants to do more than small character parts in films, to be better known. He wants to do more serious stage work, too, but no one ever asks him to do that.

'There isn't much on offer at the moment, Jemima. You know how things are. All the theatre work is so... well, trying to be cutting edge.' What was Elle trying to say? That I was out of fashion? I could do classic theatre, Shakespeare and all that. Something at the National, maybe...

'It would be great to see you on stage.'

I look round, and see Kim standing just behind me. Elle and George look amused by her comment.

'The chefs are ready to serve dinner, when you're ready, Ms Eden. We've set two more places.'

I let out an impatient sigh. Kim should know better than to interrupt me when I am talking to Elle. Across the lawn, I see Rory leaning in to talk to that girl – I still can't believe he invited her. Elle and George are now walking towards a group of men, near the bar.

'Too soon, Kim. I'll tell you when I'm ready.'

This was *my* night, and it would work on my terms. Really, people needed to remember that they were all here for me.

SIX

KIM

It seemed like no one at the party liked each other very much. The conversation was all about impressing each other, being the loudest, most confident. Jemima's agent, Elle, had a weird, high-pitched laugh, which she used often, especially when George was talking.

It was getting late when they all went inside to eat. I could see the chefs were getting impatient, worried that the food would spoil, and I wondered if I should say something to Jemima, but I knew I'd only get my head bitten off again. Eventually, the guests made their way to the dining room.

Jemima took her place at the head of the table, looking, I have to say, stunning in the gold sparkly dress. Candlelight made her pale skin look warm, glowing. Would I ever have that sort of look – so polished and expensive? Oh hell, I was meant to get a photo of her in that dress. It was too late now, she wouldn't want me taking one of her after the party. Would she shout at me, for forgetting that?

George took his seat at the far end of the table, and I could see him chatting happily to the man near him, who was about his age. I watched as Jemima held court at her end, as the starters were served, leaning towards Rory who was sat nearest to her, laughing along with Elle, including everyone in the conversation, the perfect hostess.

I stood discreetly at the side of the room, watching them all get fed – tiny course after beautiful, tiny course – I told myself it was in case I was needed, but really it was because I didn't want to miss a thing. It was a great spot to watch them all. I had never been this close to so many famous people before. What was their secret? What was it about them that made people in this room so successful? Some special quality, a star power?

I watched Jemima laughing with her friends, looking radiant, so confident. I would have done anything to be like her. She had it all – beauty, talent, success, a wonderful husband, and all this wealth. What would it take to become like that?

SEVEN

JEMIMA

Cassie – Rory's date – has clearly had work done. Her lips are so fake, and her eyelashes... Well, she looks like a baby cow, with a huge head on a tiny body. She has absolutely nothing to say of any interest – all she has contributed to the evening, so far, is to fawn over Rory and laugh at George's stupid stories. Well, if she's happy to give George attention, then that's one less task for me. Stupid girl. George is in no position to help her career.

Oh, George. I watch him at the far end of the table. All that alcohol is making him look a mess. His face is even more red and bloated than usual. It's amazing to me that I once found him attractive.

'So, working on anything new and exciting, Jemima?' Scott calls out from the middle of the table. We haven't worked together since that serial killer thing, but George likes him, and so here he is. The inevitable question.

'I've been approached about a potential film. Quite big, Netflix...'

That gets a few appreciative nods from around the table. I glance at Elle. 'But not sure that one is going to work out. Schedules, timing, you know...' Elle stares down at her plate, adjusts her napkin. *OK, it was a no, Elle, but you could back me up here?* I had to say something. And these things do sometimes change.

'A few other scripts on their way. Elle is on it, I'm sure.' I look at her again.

'It's so hard right now. So many actors trying to break onto the scene,' Scott adds. What the hell did he mean by that? That I'm past it in some way? He can hardly talk. What has he done that's any good in the past year or two? Fuck all.

'I saw you in that film!' Cassie bursts in, too loud, looking at Scott. 'You know...' she looks at Rory, as if willing for him to help her.

'*Cold Diamond,*' Scott answers, delighted to mention his most successful film. 'We are hoping to do a sequel.'

'Yes! You should. A huge commercial success. How is Brian?' George chimes in.

'Oh, same old. You know Brian... Hey, you and I should take him out! You know, a *real* night out...' The two men laugh loudly at that, and I notice George glance at me. I don't want to know what those two consider 'a real night out', but if it keeps George away from me for a few nights, that's just fine with me.

'Can we serve dessert, madam?' I look up to see one of the waiters hovering alongside me. He has excellent cheekbones. *Very nice.*

'Yes, sure, bring it in now.' I doubt anyone will eat anything sweet – not Cassie or Elle for a start. Obsessively thin, both. It will be fun to see them try and avoid it though. No doubt George will hoover up anything put in front of him. He's growing quite the belly. That old Turnball & Asser shirt he insisted on wearing is clearly struggling to stay buttoned.

I look at Rory. Now, he knows what a gym is for. His six-pack is something else. I pour myself another glass of wine and sit back in my chair. At last I can relax, and observe my guests. I could ask the waiter to top up everyone's glasses again, too, but part of me is ready for them to leave. What time is it? I've made my point to Elle, so the rest of the evening seems superfluous.

I notice a movement in the shadows of the room. Kim, standing in the corner. Why is she standing over there? I watch as the waiter with good cheekbones goes over to talk to her. Such a strange-looking girl. Almost albino, in this low light.

'Kim!' I beckon her over.

Startled, she rushes to my side. I like that. Eager to be helpful.

I clap my hands to get attention. 'Everyone. This is Kim, my new assistant. Kim, say hello to everyone.' *Oh god*, I think, *don't stoop, Kim, you look like Uriah Heep.* 'If you can't get hold of me, do try Kim. She's been absolutely brilliant today, helping organise everything.' I beam around the table. It's nice to show my softer side.

Kim looks surprised, and then smiles. I can see everyone smiling back at her, and saying loud hellos. It feels good, being the cool boss.

'Kim here is an aspiring actor!' George said loudly.

What the hell? I turn to look at Kim. 'You didn't say...'

She nods. 'Well, when I was at school.'

I study her carefully. I've read her CV, and she hadn't mentioned anything about acting on there. The bar work, the cleaning, the temping work, yes, but not an interest in acting. Why hasn't she mentioned it before?

'Join the club! I'm still trying to make it as an actor, too!' Rory calls out, causing laughs around the table. 'It's a terrible business, Kim. Why on earth don't you do something more worthwhile? Cybersecurity, wasn't it, the government told us to try?' George and Cassie love that, laughing a little too loudly.

'Seriously, we should help her! I mean, gathered here we have actors, directors, a TV presenter...' George says. 'An agent, of course...' He looks at Elle. 'Do you have an agent, Kim?'

George leans back in his chair, looking very pleased with himself.

'No... um, sorry,' Kim replies, looking completely out of her depth. She's so mousey, so quiet – hardly actor material. George really is insufferable, putting her on the spot like this.

'Is that something you can help with, Elle?' God, why was George persisting with this? I realise with a jolt that it's to irritate *me*, of course.

'Well, George, I barely have time for the clients I do have.' Elle looks awkward. *Yes, she has that right*. She isn't looking after me properly, let alone if she takes on yet more clients. 'But I do have a new, junior agent, who is very ambitious. Very talented. Leoni.' She looks up at Kim. 'I can put you in touch with her if you like?'

'Would you? I don't know... I haven't acted for a little while.' Kim glances at me. What, is she asking for my approval? She isn't getting it from me. I stare into my wine glass, taking a large swig.

Elle continues. 'Get in touch with my office. Send anything you have taped. I can ask Leoni to take a look.' She beams at George, and then me. I turn away, sharply.

'Bravo! Thank you, Elle. You see, everyone? This is how we make things work in this industry. Paying it forward.' George is clearly delighted with himself. 'Now, Kim, I'm sure Jemima doesn't need you hovering around here. It's late! Go home! No need to work so hard.'

Kim thanks him, and walks out of the room without a backward glance at me. I glare at George, who I realise, is already watching me carefully, a half-smile on his face.

EIGHT

KIM

Oh my god, oh my god! I can't believe that just happened.

I ran down to the basement, hardly able to believe my luck.
George had introduced me to an acting agent. And not just any
agent – the Elle Lobina Agency was famous! They represented
all the big names, loads of people you would know. That new
agent Elle mentioned would get in touch with me, wouldn't
she? If her boss told her to. Yes, I felt sure she would, as Elle had
promised in front of all those people. Or was I meant to call her?
I wasn't sure, but I'd work it out tomorrow.

I'd dreamed my whole life for a chance like this. It should
all have been so different. Finish school, get into drama school,
get agent, get work. That was how I had wanted my life to go.
But I had messed up at school, due to Mum... and it had all gone
downhill from there. But now! I was so right to take this job.
Look what had just happened. I wanted to jump around,
scream out loud. *Hold it together, Kim. They'll hear you
upstairs. No, do as you're told, and head home. Be the good PA.*

I changed out of my dress and hung it up. I'd feel stupid
going home on the bus dressed like that; I'd stand out too much.
Back into my jeans and sweatshirt. Better leave round the back

so I don't risk bumping into any of the guests leaving. Jemima wouldn't like that.

Outside, one of the chefs was leaning against the wall, still in his chef whites, vaping. Damian the blue-eyed server appeared next to him, bottle in hand. He grinned as I walked past him.

'Hey, Kim. What's the rush? Want a drink?'

Suddenly, that seemed like a really good idea. I was celebrating right? 'I do. Thanks.'

Damian held out the bottle to me. 'Brandy. Those rich fuckers won't even notice it's gone.'

'Thanks.' I took a swig. It slipped down so smoothly, warming my throat, burning, in a weirdly pleasant way.

'So, what's your job here?' he asked, taking back the bottle. I noticed he didn't wipe the neck after me, before taking another long swig. He'd removed his black jacket to reveal very toned arms, sleeves rolled to the elbows. 'Some sort of assistant, right?'

'PA, yes. To Jemima Eden.'

'She seems like a stuck-up bitch.'

'Can be, yes...' I said, under my breath.

'I would though, wouldn't you?' the chef smirked at Damian. 'Did you see that Cassie Armstrong? She presented that reality show on Channel 4. More my type.'

Another chef appeared in the door, holding a plate of canapes. 'With that guy from the Bond films?' He shook his head. 'He's way too old for her.'

'Well, you might be younger, but you don't have his money, mate.' The men laughed, and helped themselves to the food. I realised that I was starving, too.

'Can I have one please?' I asked.

'Help yourself. Smoked salmon. It will all go in the bin otherwise.'

Wow, delicious. Tiny orange beads decorated the salmon, and popped as I bit into them. I took another drink of brandy, and felt the tension in my shoulders start to melt away. The evening had all gone so well and I could finally relax. I felt more at home with these three than the people in there. Damian told us stories of trying to make it in acting, the walk-on parts, the recalls, what it was like at his drama school. At some point, I found myself sitting very close to him, our legs touching. *Could I?* It had been a while since I'd had sex with someone I actually liked. I was dying to tell him that I had a meeting lined up with an agent, but a part of me felt like if I said it out loud, it would vanish.

We could hear people leaving out the front, car doors banging, guests shouting goodbye. It got later, and was now colder outside. I really needed to leave, too. I didn't want Jemima spotting me, wondering what I was still doing here.

'I need to go,' I said to my new friends, a little reluctantly. It was pretty dark now.

'Steady...' I heard the men laugh as I stumbled. I put my hand against the wall to support myself.

'Let me help you,' Damian appeared next to me, and I felt his arm around me, helping me stand.

It would take me ages to get back to Max's flat. I felt so tired, the thought of travelling all that way on the night bus, and then to walk into what? Max's dickhead friends sleeping on the sofa, filling the kitchen, drinking... A wave of exhaustion swam over me. Just one more night wouldn't hurt, would it?

I found myself at the door to the basement, with Damian right behind me. I pushed it open, and watched the light illuminate the room and all its shabby furnishings.

'This is creepy,' I heard him say.

'I usually stay upstairs. Don't want to wake anyone...' I lied.

'It will do,' Damian replied, turning me towards him.

I felt his arms wrap tightly around my body, and his face so close to mine, and he smelled good, and then we were kissing, his hands in my hair, pulling me towards him. We staggered towards the sofa, and fell onto it together, the arm of it banging the back of my head. His hands snaked inside my skirt, and he kissed my neck, his stubble scratching my face. George's face appeared in my mind, his eyes, crooked smile... I shook the image away, and tried to focus on Damian, his eyes now closed, focused, as he entered me.

It was still dark outside. *Good.* My neck felt stiff from sleeping on the sofa, and I stretched, trying to ease out the tension. How much had I drunk? My head swam and I gripped the armrest to steady myself. More than anything, I wanted to lie back down, but no... I had to get up. Sunday morning and there was no way I should be here, in this house. If I was careful, Jemima and George would still be asleep and they wouldn't know I'd stayed here again.

I badly needed a shower but a quick splash of water on my face at the corner basin would have to do. I pulled on my clothes, and tied my hair back.

'Morning, madam.' A cleaner, dressed in a pale green shirt dress, earbuds in, putting out rubbish, nodded at me as I emerged from the basement.

'Hi. Sorry. Don't want to get in your way.'

'Madam.' She nodded, moving away. I wanted to correct her, and say, 'No, I'm like you. My mum was a cleaner, too,' but she was humming quietly to herself, lost in her own world.

My stomach growled. It wouldn't harm to get some food would it? Had no idea what would be open out there on a Sunday morning. The kitchen was just a few steps away. As expected, the fridge was piled with containers of food, leftovers from last night, plus all the usual things that Jemima and George liked. I pulled out a plastic box of canapés and placed them carefully in my bag. Would have cost me a fortune if I'd bought all this. The cleaner ignored me as I left.

. . .

It was too early for the usual visitors, so it was just me and Mum in the cemetery. I was excited to tell her my news. I lay my sweatshirt on the ground and unpacked my picnic.

'So, my boss had a dinner party last night, Mum. You'd have loved it. Everyone was so glamorous! There was that actor you like, Rory Jackson. I think Jemima has a thing for him. But he had his girlfriend with him. You won't know her – she presents a reality TV show; you don't like that stuff. Look, they had these little canapes, smoked salmon, and this is caviar apparently; I'm not sure what you would think of that. They won't even miss it. You loved salmon, didn't you, Mum?'

I pulled a few long strands of grass away from her head-stone. The little rose bush looked a bit bare, just one flower. Maybe I should have replaced it with something that had more colour, and less spiky. Mind you, Mum had liked roses.

'But the best thing, Mum, is that Jemima's agent was there. Elle Lobina, she's called. She's really well-known in the business. Older than I thought, too. Anyway. George, he's Jemima's husband. Did I tell you that? He's an actor, too. But you wouldn't know him, because he does films where he's playing an alien or an ape, that sort of thing. Good-looking in real life. He introduced me to everyone! Just called me over. And then the agent woman said she'd put me in touch with someone who works for her. Can you believe it! After all this time, I might get into acting after all. You know how much I wanted that.

'Oh, Mum, I wish you were here to talk this through, properly. You'd wanted this for me for so long. I know how hard you worked to pay for my Saturday dance lessons. The extra cleaning clients you took on. You were so excited whenever I did a play at school. Always there, near the front, so proud of me.'

Vivien Conner

1971–2023

Beloved Mum to Kim Conner

I sighed. Vivien. Named after Vivien Leigh, Grandma's favourite actress. We'd always loved the glamour of show business. The stars, the red carpet, the dazzling outfits, our trips to the cinema and pantomime, the escapism of it all. You'd wanted all that for me. We always went to see a show on your birthday or mine. It was the only time we could justify the price of the tickets. You hadn't got the chance to have acting lessons, or dance or singing lessons, but that hadn't stopped you, always singing around the house, making up your own songs, writing stories. If you hadn't had me, you might have found a way to make it work. For your own dreams to come true. I had to make this opportunity work.

For you, Mum.

NINE

JEMIMA

The dinner party plays on repeat in my head. It's Wednesday now, four days since the dinner party, and still no word from Elle on anything new. Cassie was so drunk when she left, she could barely stand, and it was embarrassing watching Rory have to help her into the car. Rory texted the next day to say how fabulous I looked, so that was something at least.

I pour a tiny shot of vodka into my green smoothie. That improves the flavour *immensely*. What I really need is a full body massage; that will perk me up.

Where is Kim? She can book something in for me, maybe a day spa somewhere. I can get a whole range of treatments, and it will get me out of here for a while. I can have one of those laser facials. I always feel better after one of those – fresher, younger. I text Kim, and lay back on the bed. Maybe I should get one of those little gongs so I can summon her more easily. So easy to lose someone in this huge house.

'Hi, Jemima. What can I do for you?'

Kim appears in the doorway. She looks different somehow. Is it the clothes? I don't mind her wearing a few of my cast-offs.

Has she put on a bit more make-up perhaps? Her hair is up, which suits her.

Nothing more has been said about George's ridiculous stunt at the party. Putting Elle on the spot like that. As if she would want to sign my assistant as an actor! She has hundreds of potential actors fresh out of drama school bombarding her with CVs every day of the week! He really can be clueless sometimes.

'Can you book me into Shambhala? Massage, facial, the works. Make sure you get Javona for the facial. No one else.'

'For when?'

'Today. I can get there for noon.'

'Today? That's very short notice. I can try.'

Try? Honestly, she has no idea what a valuable customer I am to them. I feel my irritation bubble up.

'They will find space for me. Thank you so much, Kim.'

TEN

KIM

I paused in the doorway. *Look at her, just lying there!* I hadn't stopped all morning, running around, doing her admin, sorting out the mess in her office. I desperately wanted to ask Jemima about her agent. I hadn't heard anything from her, and it had been days since the dinner party. I was worried that the junior agent didn't know how to get hold of me. George had gone away again, so I couldn't ask him. A worrying thought occurred to me. If they had emailed Jemima to ask for my CV, or to set up a meeting with me, would she have passed it on? I couldn't let this chance pass.

'Will do. Sorry. I'll make sure I get you into Shambala.' I smiled my most charming smile. It was now or never.

'Jemima. At your party... your agent said that she might be able to help me.'

I took a deep breath. *Just ask, Kim.* 'Have you heard anything?'

She stared at me. I recognised that look from the spy thriller I'd seen. I'd been playing catch-up, watching some of her old films on my laptop, in the evenings. She was good. No doubt about it. Jemima could do a good, irritated stare. And I was experiencing it right now.

'George shouldn't have asked Elle. That was very awkward for everyone.'

I swallowed. So, she didn't like it. I should have guessed.

Jemima sat up on the bed, still looking at me. 'You didn't tell me you were an *actor*.'

'It was what I wanted to do, when I was at school.'

Jemima swung her legs off the bed, and stood up. 'Is that why you took this job? To try and get some contacts?' She turned away from me, and walked over to the window.

What was I meant to do? Apologise? No. I had done nothing wrong here. She had everything. Success. Money. This amazing life. I wasn't a threat to her. I was just me. Kim, a nobody. Would it hurt her to give me a break, to help me out? *Stay calm, Kim.*

'That wasn't my plan. I just needed a job. I'd given up on acting, really. George was being kind, I think.'

On the table, her phone pinged. I watched as a slow smile formed on Jemima's face. Whoever had just messaged her, had clearly said something she liked. Ignoring me, she tapped away, then threw the phone down, with a satisfied flourish.

Jemima turned to look at me, as if considering her words carefully. 'Yes, kind... perhaps.'

She walked over to the sofa and perched on the arm, crossing her legs carefully at the ankles. Her foot tapped slowly.

'I could help you. If that's what you want. How old are you?'

'Twenty-three.'

'Twenty-three... I remember that age very well. You don't have an agent already?'

I shook my head.

'Why not?'

Was she really interested? It was hard to tell with Jemima.

She could have just been toying with me, amusing herself. She'd never shown any interest in my life before.

'I tried for drama school. But there was no way I could afford it.' That was partly true anyway. 'My mum was very ill. Cancer.' I looked at the floor, swallowed. I realised she was waiting for me to continue. 'She needed me. At the end of my last year at school, just before my exams, she... she... died.' I glanced up at her, to see how my lines had landed.

'Ah. I see.'

It had all been so awful. I blinked away tears. *Don't cry in front of Jemima. Hold it together.* She didn't want to see that.

'Quite the origin story.' Jemima got up, and walked back to her phone. Picked it up. Not looking at me. 'In many ways, you remind me of me. When I was your age. OK. I'll call Elle. See what's happening. Now, run along. I need that massage. See if you can book me in to stay the night too – might as well get the full benefits.'

'You don't have any availability?' *Oh god, Jemima will kill me if I can't get the treatments she wants. And I really need her to be on side, right now.* 'Please. It's for Jemima Eden. She's a regular there.'

'Oh! You should have said.' It was miraculous – the woman's tone changed in an instant.

'Yes. She wants a room, too.'

'One or two nights?'

I had no idea. 'One, I think?'

'Not a problem. All booked for Ms Eden. I will email over the confirmation. Let me give you a different phone number for next time. It will go direct to our manager. We can always find space for our VIP guests.'

Wow. So that's what it's like when you're famous. Jemima would be pleased. I was starting to get a handle on this job.

. . .

'I'm expecting a courier package from Elle later. A script. You OK to wait here to sign for it? Not sure when it might arrive.'

Jemima was standing in the hallway, with a surprisingly large bag for one night away. Surely she only needed a swimsuit, and maybe a change of clothes? But what did I know; I'd never been to a spa.

'Of course.' I was in no rush to leave anyway. 'Would she not email it?' I asked, curious. As soon as the words left my mouth, I regretted it.

To my surprise, Jemima smiled. 'It's for a TV show. All very hush-hush. They keep tight security and all the scripts are numbered, to stop them getting into the wrong hands.'

'Oh, great! That sounds promising.' No wonder she was in a good mood. This sounded like a great work opportunity for her.

'Mmm. Let's hope so. OK. I think I've got everything. I'd say call me if any problems, but actually, don't. I will be back tomorrow and I could do with the break. I am sure you can manage.' And with that, she was gone, door slamming behind her.

I sat on the stairs and exhaled. The house was eerily quiet with just me in it. No George stomping around, or Jemima's music playing from her office. The cleaners had long gone and wouldn't be in until seven tomorrow morning. I had a few emails to reply to, and of course, at some point the courier would arrive, but otherwise, I could relax.

I waited until I knew Jemima had driven away, and had definitely not forgotten anything, and went into the kitchen to make myself a coffee. I took my cup over to the sofa in the window, and lay down. Now, this was the life. It was almost as if the house was mine. And for one night, it was. If only Mum could see me now.

I was making myself a snack, when a loud buzz sounded

from the door security system. I thanked the man, took the padded envelope from him, and closed the door. I took it up to Jemima's office and placed it on her desk. Like the good assistant I am, I texted her:

> Script arrived safely. Have a great time.

Time to leave. I paused in the hallway. Right now, I had the place to myself. I didn't actually need to go back to Max's tonight. I could stay in the basement and no one would know. Hell, I could stay in one of the bedrooms and no one would know.

I decided to find some proper blankets, and maybe a decent pillow to make my night on the basement sofa a little more comfortable. Upstairs was a huge airing cupboard, organised with printed labels on the shelves, which contained a choice of towels, and quilts, all so luxurious. I could see the door to the main bathroom, just along the landing, was open. Inside was a huge roll-top bath, big enough for two.

When was the last time I'd had a bath? We just had a shower at Max's and you didn't want to spend much time in there – best not to look too closely at the dirt between the tiles and the mould growing on the ceiling. This bathroom, by contrast, was how I imagined a luxury hotel. On a shelf behind the bath sat rows of oils in such pretty glass bottles, labelled with Moroccan rose, ambre, vanilla, frankincense... No one would ever know.

As the steaming hot water filled the bath, I smelled each of the bottles in turn. This one was my favourite, so delicious. I poured the oil into the water, and watched it turn to bubbles. Leaving my clothes in a pile next to me, I stepped in, and let my body sink down into the hot, silky water. Oh my god. It smelled divine. I felt my neck relax against the rim of the bath. I could stretch out in all directions! Pure bliss. I felt all the tension start

to leave my body. This is what it felt like to live here, to be
Jemima. Would I ever have a place like this? In that moment, I
started to believe, that yes, just maybe, one day I would.

ELEVEN

KIM

Jemima returned the next afternoon in a very good mood, practically singing as she came in and dumped her bag on the floor. Was I meant to deal with it? Unpack? The boundaries of my job had never really been made clear. She was so excited to read her script she almost ran up the stairs.

It *was* a good script. It wasn't a huge part for her, but it was a good part, playing the lady of the manor. The sort of things that Americans love, and gets shown on a primetime Sunday evening. I could see her in the role; it would suit someone with her red hair, her look. Yes, of course I read it. I'm sure you would have, too. It was just lying there, in her office, and it was very easy to gently open the envelope, take a few photos on my phone, and then ease it back inside after I'd finished. I'd barely creased the pages.

The spa emailed through her bill. Before I arrived, Jemima's admin had been in a right mess. Receipts for nutritional supplements, clothes, catering, wine deliveries, stylists... her previous PA had clearly done nothing with all this, and the accountant had been chasing. Apparently, it all counted as 'business expenses' – even hair and spa treatments. Her personal trainer was charging her £150 an hour! It made my salary look paltry by comparison.

As I was about to file the spa invoice, I noticed something. A beer? Jemima doesn't drink beer. There are usually some in the fridge, sure, but I'm sure she said something about how gluten made her bloated. Who was that for? Come to think of it, there was a lot of food for one person. *Well, well, Jemima. Who did you meet at the spa?* She had never mentioned a friend. But she'd have said, wouldn't she? A man? Rory? She had kept a very close eye on him at the dinner. But he had that girlfriend, who was much younger than Jemima.

A phone call to the work phone interrupted my thoughts.

Max popped into my head. But, no, he doesn't have this number. I hadn't been back to the flat for a couple of days and he had been sending me increasingly irate texts. This month's rent was overdue, but I knew he could afford it more than me. Let him stew a bit longer, make up for the loud parties, and the assholes he had let have sex in my room.

'Is this Kim? Hi. Leoni. From the Elle Lobina Agency.'

Oh my god! Jemima had been true to her word. She had contacted her agent. 'Yes, that's me.'

'Jemima gave us this number. Says you are looking for a new agent.' Well, my first agent, but I wasn't going to draw attention to that. 'Can you send me your headshots, CV, anything else you have... showreel, that sort of thing? Jemima said you haven't done much professional work yet...'

I gulped. I hadn't done *any* professional work. I hadn't done any acting since school. I was over my head, here. But I had absolutely nothing to lose.

'Sure, that's really kind of you. I can send you all that. Thank you, I really appreciate this.'

A pause at the end of the line. 'OK. Great. Send those things over, and then why don't you come in for a chat?'

'Great! I can do any day this week.' *Too eager, desperate.* I needed to calm down, as if I had loads of options, rather than just one.

'Tomorrow? After three?' *So soon?*

'Love to! Thanks so much!'

I pressed end on the call, and had to resist the urge to jump around the room, screaming. I was going to see an agent! Surely, they would want to take me on, because Jemima had contacted them? Maybe they saw it as a favour? Whatever, I was going to try and make the best of this chance. Now I had to get my act together, take some selfies, record a monologue or two. That part I could do. I could still remember the script I'd helped Jemima to learn, so I could do that. I needed to prepare!

TWELVE

KIM

'What on earth is going on here?'

I turned around to find Jemima standing in the doorway, taking in the scene: the towels covered in red blotches all over the floor, me, looking like a startled rabbit, hair dripping wet.

'Dying my hair. Sorry, didn't think you'd mind…'

'Why the hell are you doing that here?'

I scrabbled around on the floor, picking up the evidence. 'I'm so sorry, Jemima. I wanted to do it at home this morning, but my flatmate had used all the hot water. I'm meeting that new agent later, and wanted to look my best. It won't happen again.'

'I heard you down here. I need you to run through my lines with me.'

I could see her taking it all in. Thank god I had tidied up my nightshirt, pillow and blankets. *That was close.*

'Of course. I will be up in a moment.'

'I don't want anything like this to happen again, am I understood? This is a place of work, not a salon. This is very unprofessional, Kim.'

My eye fell on the toothbrush lying on the bathroom sink,

the door just open enough to see in there. I willed Jemima to look the other way, to leave. She mustn't know that I'd been staying here. Not now. I couldn't lose this job now.

'See you upstairs.' Jemima closed the door behind her, and I let out a relieved sigh. That was foolish and stupid, almost getting caught, but I knew I had to make the most of this chance, and I wanted to be memorable.

I quickly combed my hair and dried it the best I could using an old towel. I knew I had to rush to get upstairs, but I couldn't resist a quick peek in the mirror. Yes. It had worked! A delicious dark red colour. I couldn't wait to see what it looked like when it dried properly.

I had spent ages choosing the right colour, the best one to get the closest match. It did look good with my eyes! It made their pale blue, almost-lilac colour really stand out. Plenty of black mascara and I would look just right for my interview later. Long, dark red hair. Just the same as Jemima. No more boring Kim, with my ordinary hair. A new Kim. Better.

For all her experience, for all her years in the business, I knew something that most people didn't: Jemima Eden was really bad at learning lines. No matter how many times we went through her script that morning, she just wasn't getting it right. Some of the lines were OK, but she was saying them in the wrong places, not getting the cues. She blamed me of course.

'You said it differently last time! Go from the bit where I talk about my son.'

We went back to the start of the page. It must have been three hours since we started working. This was madness. She needed to take a break, chill out a bit. I glanced at the clock.

'Am I boring you, Kim?'

'No! Sorry. It's just that—'

'What, you need lunch?' She threw her script on the piano

and stretched her arms above her head. 'I guess I do, too. I get so lost in the moment. Can you go and get two salads for us? Then we can run through again. We can eat in here.'

Oh god, how long did she want to do this for? 'No, it's just that... I need to get to the agency for three. For my meeting.' Had Jemima forgotten? I had told her this morning that my meeting was today.

'Today? I'm sorry, Kim. Can you delay it, please. This has to take priority.'

I felt my pulse quicken. She couldn't be serious. 'I did tell you—'

Jemima shook her head. 'Sorry. This tape has to happen today. We can have lunch, then set up the camera. Elle won't mind. You can go tomorrow when I've sent this off.'

But if I don't go today, then I was messing the agent, Leoni, around, and there was no guarantee she would want to see me again. What if she thought me rude or arrogant for cancelling?

I could call Leoni and try to tell her that Jemima needed me to work, and she might understand. Or she might not. I might get labelled as unreliable, not ready to turn up for castings or rehearsals when needed. I didn't want to mess this up before I'd even really started.

I took a deep breath and chose my words carefully. 'You seem ready to me. You are so good at the lines. We could try and do a recording now, while its fresh. And then I could leave on time...'

She stared at me, incredulous. 'I'll tell you when I'm ready. Your job is to help me. This is important.'

This was bullshit. Jemima was a huge star. If she wanted to send her tape tomorrow, that would be just fine. It was people like me who didn't get chances like this every day. I stood my ground. 'It's better not to over-rehearse. Let's record it now.'

'Oh so, you're the expert now, are you?' Jemima looked at

me, then crossed her legs, resting one, slim arm on her sofa. 'Remind me, just *how* many acting jobs have you done?'

There wasn't much I could say to that.

'I have worked in this industry for *years*. You don't get to tell me how to do my job.'

'Now, ladies. What's going on here? Cross words? What sort of welcome home is this?' Behind me, George appeared in the doorway.

Jemima leaned back on the sofa, folded her arms. 'You're back.'

George walked past me, and leaned over Jemima, pulling her into an awkward hug. 'My meeting went well, thanks for asking.'

'I have a very important self-tape to do and Kim, here, has better places to be.'

George turned and smiled at me. 'Do you? How exciting.' I couldn't help but smile back at him.

'A meeting. With Leoni, at Elle's agency.'

'Oh good! Fantastic. So, Elle did listen to me. And, I know I'm a man and can't be relied on to notice these things, but you look different! Another redhead! How fantastic!' He turned to look at Jemima. 'I'm sure we can manage, darling? I'm here now. Kim can run along, can't she?'

I looked from one to the other. Jemima looked furious. I watched her take a moment.

'I need someone I can rely on, George. Kim is here to help me, and this is important.' I noticed that her voice had changed completely. No longer angry, she used a sweeter voice with him. I had never heard her sound like that, but it seemed to work.

'I agree with you, of course, darling. But we don't want to mess around the agency, either. And it was us that set this up. Look, I can help you do the self-tape. Good for us to spend this time together. I might need a coffee first though.' George dumped his jacket on the arm of the sofa.

Did that mean I could leave?

'Is this the script?' George walked over to the piano and picked it up. I glanced over at Jemima, but she focused on him. If I was lucky, an Uber would still get me there on time, if I went right now. I didn't want to spend the money, but I couldn't risk the bus. *Go now, Kim.*

'OK, I'll head off now...'

I was in the hallway, pulling on my jacket, when Jemima appeared, and slowly folded her arms. She held my gaze, and spoke quietly. 'Kim. This isn't working out. Leave your keys. And work phone.'

Was she firing me?

'I'm sorry. I can be back later if you still need to practise. I do need this job.'

Every day I seemed to end up apologising to her. Nothing I did was ever right. She was impossible to please.

'It probably won't take more than an hour, half an hour, probably. I can come straight back...' I pleaded.

'Let me spell this out for you, Kim. I need one hundred percent commitment. I can't have my assistant running off to castings and meetings in the middle of the day. This simply isn't working out. You're fired.' And with that, she turned and left me standing there.

THIRTEEN

KIM

I stood outside, trying to catch my breath. What had I done wrong? This job was crazy, but it was the best-paid job I had ever had. And in some ways, working here had become a refuge, being able to stay there a few times, I could almost imagine that my life was better, like theirs. How could she do that to me? Jemima Eden had everything, so much privilege, and she had treated me like I was disposable.

I thought of that receipt for the spa. It would have been so easy to forward that to George and he would work out the rest, ask Jemima who had been at the spa with her. But I hadn't done that – I'd been loyal to Jemima, and for what? So she could fire me anyway? He deserved so much better than that witch.

I walked fast down the road, tapping my phone, trying to choose the fastest Uber. I could have lied, told Jemima I was going to the doctor, had a hospital appointment, and she couldn't have objected to that, could she? But no, I had been honest, telling her I was going to the agency. I cursed myself. *You need to act smarter, Kim. Never forget that people are mostly looking out for themselves.* I stopped still. A thought occurred to me... was that it? Was Jemima *jealous* of me? No, that made no sense. I was a nobody.

I made it to the Elle Lobina agency with seconds to spare. I stopped to take a few deep breaths, and let go of some of the tension from earlier. Screw her. I would show Jemima that I didn't need that poxy job. This meeting with Leoni had to work. You never know, maybe she would sign me, and then I'd never have to work as a PA again.

I pressed the discreet gold button set into a panel by the door, and was buzzed into a spacious, modern waiting room filled with brightly coloured chairs. Framed posters of films lined the walls. Faces of household names looked down on me, the agency's most famous clients. I recognised a man from a war film I'd hated. And a woman... she'd been in that Netflix series. And there, staring down at me, a black-and-white portrait of Jemima Eden, looking like the star that she was. What was I doing here? I was completely out of my league.

'Hello? Can I help you?' The receptionist called over to me.

'Sorry. Hi. Kim Conner. I'm here to see Leoni Hilton.'

He studied me through his over-sized black glasses. 'I'll let her know. Take a seat.'

I was suddenly desperate to go to the toilet, to get a drink of water, but what if Leoni came out, and I wasn't here? *No, take a seat, sit down, try and stay calm.*

'Hello?'

I looked up. I recognised her at once from Jemima's dinner party. Elle Lobina. I jumped up and held out my hand to shake hers. Elle looked amused, and I let my hand fall back down.

'Your Jemima's assistant, yes? We met at her dinner party. You look different...'

My hand went up to my hair. 'Yes, I coloured my hair. Is that OK?'

Elle studied me for a moment. 'Yes. It's just that... goodness. You look so like Jemima. When we first met. It's the long red hair. It suits you.'

She smiled at me warmly. 'You here to see Leoni? She's very good. You'll be in safe hands with her.' Elle turned to walk away, and then added, 'Say hi to Jemima for me.'

FOURTEEN

JEMIMA

'You can't fall out with everyone. It makes you look like a total bitch.'

'She gives me the creeps. Did you see her hair? She has dyed her hair to look like me! It's so weird.'

'She doesn't look anything like you. That's insane. She's a good ten years younger for a start.'

'Fuck you.'

'Now, Jemima, darling. Don't give me a hard time. I'm shattered. I don't appreciate coming home and walking into another domestic drama.'

'I've fired her, so that's one domestic drama you don't need to worry about.'

George shuts the fridge and looks at me. 'Now, that's silly. You can't just keep getting rid of people. How many assistants is that now? Is Kim number four? And then you complain you don't have anyone to help you.'

'I can manage.'

He lets out a heavy sigh. I know what that means. I'm about to get a lecture.

'It's good for you to have someone here when I'm away.'

George sighs again, and runs his hand through his hair. I used to love it when he did that. 'It's safer having someone here. I worry about you, alone in this big old house.'

'It's like Fort Knox. You don't need to worry at all.'

George shakes his head. 'Have you thought what people might think? Kim has gone to the agency, hasn't she? What if she mentions that you've fired her to Elle? You don't want to get a reputation, as one of *those* actresses.' He pauses to look at me. 'You don't want to be considered *difficult*.'

Difficult? How dare he. He has no idea. It's so easy for him. No one calls men difficult. Assertive, maybe. But not difficult. I look at George, in his sweatpants and navy sweater. He used to be on my side. I take a breath. Better to try and keep the peace.

'Maybe you're right.'

He walks towards me, and takes hold of my arm.

'I'm always right, Jemima. You know that.'

FIFTEEN

KIM

'Kim? Hi!' A tiny, pixie-faced woman held out her hand. 'I'm Leoni. Thanks so much for coming in.'

Leoni looked not much older than me, and yet here she was, an agent in this swanky office. I wondered how she had got the job. Nepo baby? Or just annoyingly talented.

I followed her down a corridor, until the end, and then into a small office, with just enough space for a narrow desk and two chairs. She had a clear view of the train tracks below. So, still very much the junior here. I warmed to her a little more. Leoni edged around the desk and sat down. She indicated for me to sit.

'So. Elle said I needed to set up a meeting with you.'

'Thanks. Yes, it's really good of you.'

I watched her scan her laptop. 'Says here you did drama A-level. Is that it? No drama school? No acting work that I can see?'

'I've been working various jobs – bars, you know to get by, but really, I would love to do this.'

Leoni leaned back in her chair, studying me. 'I tend to sign people from drama school. This is very unusual. But Jemima recommended you, so here we are.'

Oh god, she hates me. She clearly doesn't want me here.

'I rather liked your monologue. It had something... raw.' She looked up, as if seeing me for the first time. 'You've got a strong look. That hair... not your real colour is it?'

I shook my head.

She shrugged. 'It works. OK. If we are doing this, first thing you need is proper headshots. Here is a list of the photographers we recommend.'

I glanced at the list. That one was based in Mayfair. What was this going to cost me?

'Get those done, send them over, and I'll see what I can do.' She stared at me. 'You do have an unusual look... that might work in your favour. Some directors are looking for untrained talent. Bit... edgy.' Leoni leaned back in her chair. 'And Jemima Eden is a very important client for us.'

So, this was for Jemima's benefit. To keep in with her. Would Leoni take me on when she found out that Jemima had fired me? It seemed unlikely. But she had seen something in me, had liked my monologue. Maybe I was in with a chance.

'That's so great. Thank you.' As I left Leoni's office and closed the door behind me, I wondered if I would ever hear from her again. Especially when she found out that I no longer worked for Jemima.

'You're back! I was starting to think you'd done a runner.' Max pounced on me as soon as I walked into the flat.

'I'll pay you as soon as I can, Max.'

'You said that two weeks ago. Look, Kim. If you can't afford it, you'll need to move out.' Max leaned against the kitchen wall.

Jemima had paid me last month and that had cleared some of my overdraft, leaving me with hardly any left.

'I'm not here that much. Can I pay less of the bills?' It was worth a try.

'It doesn't work like that. That isn't our agreement. Look, Kim. It's clear this isn't working. I've got people queuing up to live here. Time to call it a day.'

I looked around the flat, at its poky kitchen that badly needed updating. Compared to Jemima and George's home, this was a hovel.

'OK. Whatever, Max.' I pushed past him, into my room. I pulled my case from under the bed, started to fill it with my stuff. He appeared in the doorway, behind me.

'You still owe me for the bills. You can't just take off.'

'Bank of mum and dad drying up?' I replied. All that partying must cost a lot. I pulled clothes from the wardrobe. Did I really need any of this? It all looked so old, so cheap. I could ditch all this and just wear what I'd got from Jemima. Would I even be allowed back there to collect my stuff? Surely George would let me in?

'I know you can get money easily, Kim.' What the hell? I turned to look at Max.

'You know, working in the nightclub.' He smirked at me. How did he know about that? I tried not to think of that place. It was all quite easy at first, just spend a bit of time with the customers, get them to buy more drinks. One of the other girls told me how much she got for extras, and, well, it was almost like acting wasn't it? Max had no right to judge me.

'Go to hell, Max.'

I looked around the room, one last time. A few books, a cheap, fluffy blanket, and a box on the floor containing old scripts and programmes from school. A photo of me and Mum. I put that carefully in my case. I didn't need the rest of it. It belonged in the past. Max stepped back, as I pushed past him into the corridor. I dropped the key on the door mat. 'Bye, Max. Don't stay in touch.'

Other people had parents to go home to, when things didn't work out. Not me. We'd rented our whole lives, and when Mum died, that was it. Homeless. I sat in the park, my bag at my feet, trying to think. I could get a cheap room somewhere on Airbnb, for tonight, but I would soon run out of money that way. There was a quick way to make some cash, easy to find customers online, but I didn't want to ever do that again. There had to be a better way. I was worth more than stupid bar jobs, temp jobs...

Why did people like Jemima get all the luck, all the money, and people like me had to scratch around to get by? I watched two women walk past, one older. Laughing, enjoying each other's company. Were they friends? Mother and daughter? They had no idea how lucky they were. I'd lost touch with friends from school – I couldn't just turn up after not contacting them for a couple of years, and say, 'Hi! Remember me, can I stay?'

My phone rang, an unknown number.

'Kim? Is this the right number? Is that Kim?' I recognised that deep, posh voice right away. I sat up straight.

'Yes. Hi, George.'

'Good! Can you come back to the house?' He sounded stressed. I could imagine him pacing the kitchen, rubbing his head, in that way he did.

'George, you know Jemima fired me, right?' A man walking past glanced at me.

'Forget that. We need you. I need you.' He did? What on earth for?

'It's all hit the fan here. Come as soon as you can. And don't talk to any press outside.'

I stared at my phone after he hung up. Press outside? What the hell had happened?

SIXTEEN

JEMIMA

'Kim must have sold the story.'

'We don't know that. The journalist could have made it up.' George was pacing up and down the room, which just made me feel more irritated.

'Oh, it's easy for you to say. They aren't out there, stalking you, George.'

I lie on the bed, staring at the ceiling. Outside, I can hear men talking, laughing. A car beeps its horn, probably enjoying the circus outside. How did they even know where we lived? I guess one hack finds out, then they all follow, like a herd of sheep.

'Is it because I fired her? Or it could have been one of the catering staff. We hadn't had those waiters before. Who hired them? I'm going to call the caterers.' I reach for my phone.

'For chrissake, don't do that, Jemima. Elle says the best thing is to ignore it, and don't add any fuel to the fire. She's working on a statement. Let her handle this.'

I sit up to look at him. 'You know it's not true, don't you? About Rory. He's a friend, that's all. You know, it wouldn't surprise me at all if it was that Cassie. Trying to boost *her* career!'

Oh god, was it Rory who leaked the story himself? Had he decided to turn on me? To use me? The story was very light on details and just said that we had been seen out together, but that in itself was hardly evidence. Had it been someone at the spa? We had been so discreet...

George is weirdly calm, which is never a good sign. I look at him. 'You know he's just a friend, don't you?' I repeat.

It hasn't been great between me and George for a long time, and we both know that. But then, we also know that George is hardly the most innocent person here. There are so many stories about him, when he's away filming. I'd minded at first, and then stopped caring.

George speaks eventually. 'It's not Kim. That's not logical. She's gone to your agency. She wouldn't mess that up.' He might have a point there. 'And this story would have come out before you fired her.'

'Oh, make them go away, George. Please. I can't bear it.'

'I'm working on it. Police don't seem to be in any rush to get here.'

George's phone rings.

I look at him, expectantly.

'It's Kim. She's outside. I need to let her in.'

'Why the hell is she here? What if it was her? We hardly know her.'

'I can't manage all this... The phones are going wild, and your social media. We need her to come in and help. I need her to come in and help.'

I groan. 'Can't Elle send someone over? Someone from her office.'

'I think this is for us to deal with, don't you? Don't make this a bigger deal than it is already.'

I lie back on the bed, defeated.

'OK. She can come back. Just until this is over.'

SEVENTEEN

KIM

There must have been at least fifteen journalists and photographers outside the house when I arrived. I stood on the opposite side of the road, and tried to work out what to do. Jemima was trending all over social media – I had read all about it on the bus. Apparently, she was having an affair with Rory Jackson. So, was that who she was at the spa with? If so, anyone who worked at that posh spa would know what she'd been up to. He'd also been at her dinner party... but he'd left with that Cassie. Had Jemima and Rory actually just been flaunting themselves in front of George? That poor man. And now the whole world knew. I wondered how he was feeling right now. I was glad that George had reached out to me, to ask me to come back, that he trusted me with this.

The men outside looked like they had just come from a football match – bald heads, red-faced, loud and obnoxious. I thought of Jemima inside, hiding away. She barely went out as it was, and I could see why, if this was the attention she got.

I'd read these sorts of stories many times. Who hadn't? Easy clickbait while scrolling through your phone, when you were bored, slumped on the sofa. It was all part of the game, wasn't it? The deal you made when you wanted to be famous, to be known, and I was right here, seeing it play out in real life. I should try and go round the back. There was no way I could get in the front door without the press seeing me. I realised with a start that I no longer had my key. I'd left it on the hallway table, as instructed.

I could leave right now. Did I really want to go back in there, and help Jemima? After how she'd treated me? But if it meant I could keep the job and buy me some time until I signed with the agency, it was worth it. I didn't have a lot of other options right now.

I called George, who picked up fast, and said he would let me in round the back. The relief in his voice was palpable. I crossed the road briskly, and walked fast past the men, up the drive and round the back of the house.

'Hey, lady! Come and talk to us! We pay!'

I turned to look. A man smiled at me, stepped forward. I wondered, just for a moment, how much he was offering.

'Quick, come inside.' George appeared at the end of the drive and waved for me to follow him. The sound of the men shouting died away as he slammed the door shut.

'She's upstairs. I need to get back up there. Can you handle the phone calls and emails please? Just take messages from friends, anything related to work, that sort of thing. Forward me anything that I need to deal with. We'll put out a statement later, but for now, just sift out anything urgent and let me know.'

I nodded. George stood there, slightly breathless, looking a little flushed. 'Cancel Jemima's appointments for the next few days. I will try and take her away. Kim, it would be really helpful if you could stay here and keep an eye on the house. Would you be OK with that?'

'Of course. If you think that's OK. Will the press go away?' I wasn't sure I wanted to be here, with all of them outside.

'Should do. If they see us leave. It would help me a lot. She's a mess up there.'

That made sense. They wouldn't be interested in me. I glanced around the hallway. I could stay here, in the house, and without Jemima and George to deal with. I tried to think fast.

'Sure. I'll help in any way I can. Can I get you anything? A coffee?' I offered. He must be devastated about the story – finding out that Jemima had cheated on him. But he didn't look upset, exactly – more resigned. As if he was used to it, as if this had happened before.

'That's incredibly kind. Thank you. Yes, I'd love one.' He smiled, creases appearing. 'And, Kim? Jemima's bark is always worse than her bite. Your keys and phone are where you left them. I'm glad you are here.'

I felt the urge to pull him into a hug, he looked so exhausted by it all, but instead, I gave a quick nod, and watched him run up the stairs.

I took my bag down to the basement, and looked around. *So, here I am again*. If Jemima and George went away, I could stay here for a few days. Buy me some time. I exhaled. It would do for now.

But first, coffee for George. Maybe something for her ladyship, and put on my best, helpful face.

EIGHTEEN

JEMIMA

If I have to spend another night in this hotel room with George, I'll kill him. I think I'd rather go home and face the journalists. Kim told us last night that there was only one solitary photographer outside now, and it's otherwise pretty calm at the house.

'Hello, darling. You look better.' George appears in his towelling robe, his hair dripping on the carpet. 'I've ordered room service. Poached eggs. Your favourite.' He's talking to me like I'm a child.

'I'm fine.' I sit up, reach for a glass of water. My head feels like sludge. I badly need a coffee. 'Time I went downstairs.'

'Are you sure?' George sits next to me on the bed, water droplets falling on my arm. I edge away.

This room, all chintzy pale greens and swag curtains, is starting to do my head in. It might be George's idea of luxury and taste, but it's certainly not mine. Time to get up before the walls start closing in on me. I look at my bedside table.

'Did you take my phone, darling?' I'm sure I'd left it right there last night.

'Yes. It's here. I put it on charge for you.' George pulls his phone, and mine, out of his bathrobe pocket. 'Is looking at that going to help your mood?'

I take the phone from him, irritated. No messages from Rory, but of course he knows better than to message me when I'm away with George. I scroll through the news apps. Good. No longer front-page news. A girl has been murdered, poor thing. A new reality show has started and the story about me has been bumped right to the bottom of the page.

'All looks good. Horrid news about that kid, but looking good for me. Just need to get in the shower. I'll be ready to go down in ten minutes.' My head swims as I tried to stand up. *God, why do I still feel tired after sleeping so much?*

I do feel better after a shower, less groggy. My jeans slip on – I've lost weight, which is something positive out of this whole debacle. A loose blouse, hair freshly washed, and subtle make-up. A quick espresso, and I'm ready to face my audience.

The breakfast room goes quiet as we walk in, as always happens in hotels, airports, shops, wherever. I used to love it, all the attention. But then someone sells a story on you, and you start to hide away from the world...

Well, I can't hide away in that awful room forever. The old Jemima would never forgive me. I haven't done anything wrong! Sometimes, you do just need to show your face, show the world that you don't care what people are saying about you, and get on with it. I notice a man turn round and watch me walk past, his wife shooting him an irritated look. I feel George's hand on my back; he used to love these moments. Always happy to show off his famous wife, enjoying the envious looks from other men.

We're shown to a table overlooking the garden, and a very pretty tiled pool just outside. Green-and-white-striped loungers surround the pool, and it does look inviting. Maybe a very quick swim would be nice? The water looks cold, inviting. It would help to clear my head. A waiter pours coffee for me.

'Is this too soon? Everyone is watching us.' George says, passing me a croissant.

'I'm fine.'

'People might take photos of you. Everyone's staring... We should go back up to the room.'

'We are allowed to be here. Calm down, George.'

I see a look flash across his face, and then he helps himself to more coffee. We haven't got to the bottom of who sold the story of me yet, but we will. George has people looking into it. It's most likely someone at the spa hotel. I'll be going somewhere else in future, that's for sure.

Well, here I am in a hotel with my husband. Let someone share *that* story. A scene of ordinary domestic bliss, George reading his phone, me eating my yoghurt and berries. All very normal.

'Kim messaged. Apparently the coast is clear at home.' George puts his phone down as his cooked breakfast arrives. How he can eat all that disgusting processed pork is a mystery to me. Kim has been useful at least, while we'd been away. Rearranged some meetings for me, fired the cleaners, hired new ones – I couldn't risk keeping the staff we had. It could have been anyone.

Of course I've ruminated that it could have been Kim who'd sold a story on me. But George is right. She has too much to lose. And she'd come back to work, all apologetic and supportive, so it does seem unlikely to be her. I'll have to replace her soon enough in any case; she's a little weird. But right now, she will do.

George's phone buzzes, and he slides it over to me. 'Elle.'

Please don't let this be more bad news.

'Jemima! Good. It's you! I tried your phone earlier, but it went to voicemail.'

'Everything OK?'

'I think the story is dying down. So, that's a relief. Now, you know what they say, no publicity is bad publicity. We're getting a lot of interest in you. And in a good way.'

George looks at me, curious. He's clearly listening to what she's saying.

'I heard back from the film company, about that self-tape you did. I've also had some interesting emails enquiring about your availability. It seems your little trip into the gossip columns has boosted your visibility.' I glance again at George. I'm not sure he'll like how this conversation is going.

'It might be too soon, for you, of course, I would understand. You might want to let the dust settle.'

'I'm fine, Elle. Going stir-crazy here, that's for sure. Tell me everything.' So, my so-called affair with Rory has made me a little more interesting to casting directors. How interesting.

'Why don't you come for lunch? We can talk it all through. Go to one of our old haunts.'

I wasn't sure about that. Elle's office is right in the heart of Soho. It's always so busy around there.

'Jemima? I know what you're thinking. It will be fine. We can go to my club. They are so discreet. Come on, it will be like old times. You used to love going out.'

She's right, I did. We had some memorable lunches back in the early days, me and Elle, that went on late into the night. But that felt like a different time.

I turn to George. 'It's time to leave.'

ACT 2

NINETEEN

KIM

Jemima left for the airport in a whirlwind of chaos and excitement. I'd helped her pack her suitcases, printed out her boarding pass ('just in case, I don't trust the app') and packed a salad for her to take on the flight. No airport food for Jemima Eden. It was only an hour's flight to Edinburgh, where she would be met by a driver organised by the film company, who would take her straight to St Andrews. Elle's office had sent through the contracts and filming schedule earlier in the week for the historical drama she had done the tape for, and it had been all go since then. Jemima had been enthusiastic to learn her lines, and we'd worked on them late into the night. She was so excited when she got the part, but that had now morphed into her grumbling about her lack of lines. Not that she was much good at remembering the few she had.

'It's a cameo. It's a role that can steal a scene. It's a great part,' I told her. I was on my absolute best behaviour, having come so close to losing this job.

That had placated her. 'Yes, it is, and really, it's perfect. Great director, good actors, filming in Scotland…'

Jemima had been sent several scripts since the story about

her and Rory had come out, and didn't we all know about it. I was starting to think she'd planted the story herself, it had worked out so well for her.

It was a dream role for any actor – I would have loved the chance. A period drama set up in the Scottish Highlands, and Jemima was playing the owner of a baronial hall, the English wife of a Scottish laird, which was just as well, as her attempts at a Scottish accent were soon abandoned. It sounded so cool, acting in a castle. I'd seen the contract when Elle sent it through, and the money was insane for the number of lines she had. Money like that would have set me up for life.

It all seemed to distract her from the fact that she'd fired me – that was old news, now everything was going her way and I could be vaguely useful. She'd never apologised, of course. People like that never did.

There had been an awkward moment when I told her I couldn't fly up with her. I made up some story about being scared of flying. It seemed easier than trying to explain that I didn't have a passport. I didn't even have a driving licence. No ID that I could use that would get me on a plane, anyway. What if I got to the airport with Jemima, and they didn't let me get on the plane? That would be so humiliating. No, the train would be just fine. It only took five hours and then another train to St Andrews, and she could phone me if she needed me. I really needed to sort out proper ID. One for the to-do list.

'I need you with me.' Jemima had looked irritated. What on earth for? She would be surrounded by film crew, production assistants, that sort of thing.

'You can phone me right up until take-off. I've got the number of the assistant producer. She seems great.'

'It's not ideal, Kim. We start filming on Wednesday.' I watched her open her script again. Was Jemima Eden nervous?

George had seemed tense leading up to Jemima's flight. 'Is this absolutely the right timing for you, darling? It feels like, with everything that has been going on, it might just be best to pass on this one.'

'Stop fretting, George. I'm an actor, darling. This is what I do. Kim, can you get my hat please, the cashmere cream one? It'll be freezing up there.'

'I think you are rushing into this.' George hovered, blocking the hallway.

I kept myself busy, checking the bags, though I was very much listening in.

'It's been months since I worked, George. I need to do this.'

George was very still, watching Jemima as she rummaged in her bag.

'I need to go back out to LA any day. You might not be back in time.'

Jemima sighed, closed her bag, and walked over to him. 'Are you saying you will miss me, George?' She smiled her most dazzling smile.

'You know I will.'

'We can Facetime. And I'll be back before you, probably. Honestly, George. The times you've been away and I've been stuck here. You'll survive!'

'Well, don't go having an affair with any of your co-stars.'

I looked up. I couldn't believe George had just said that. Jemima didn't respond.

'I'm joking! Just trying to lighten the mood.' George stepped forward and pulled Jemima into a bear-hug. I looked away.

'Not funny.'

'You know me, the jealous type.' George kissed her, then let her go.

I felt the need to break the tension, remind them I was sitting there. 'Driver is coming at five. I've allowed plenty of time for traffic. Is that OK, Jemima?'

She looked round at me. 'Perfect. Thank you, Kim.'

TWENTY

JEMIMA

Am I making a terrible mistake? I feel unsettled leaving George and Kim behind, though I can't quite work out why. As the driver pulls into VIP parking at Heathrow, I feel a surge of adrenalin. Can I really do this? I haven't left London in a very long time.

Heathrow has an excited buzz about it, people off to new adventures, for new experiences, new people to meet. I put on my dark glasses as the driver opens the door. A family walks past me, an excited toddler straining to get out of her stroller. The mum turns to look at me. I turn my face away and followed the driver quickly through the departure hall, until a man in a waistcoat shows me through a doorway, and I'm safely tucked away in the VIP area. I let out a long exhale. No one will bother me in here.

A whirl of production people introduce themselves, their names all a blur; through security, bag checks and then I'm seated on the plane, right at the front in the window seat. *I need to calm down.* I rummage for my pills. One of these will help.

'Champagne, Ms Eden?'

'Yes, please.' A little celebration for me, for getting this part.

Elle had been right. A great cast, great director, and would get seen by millions. Vanessa was such a good role – clever, key to the whole plot, but without having a stupid number of lines to learn. I reach into my bag again. No harm in going over the lines, just so I'm word-perfect. It's irritating that Kim isn't here to read the other parts with me.

My hand shakes a little. Maybe the pills don't go so well with alcohol. *Just nerves, Jemima, take a deep breath.* Where is it...? I look inside my bag. A couple of magazines Kim has picked up for me, *The Stage*, my salad... I definitely put my script in here. I look round, panicking. Have I packed it in my suitcase instead? No, I'm sure I put it in here. I text Kim.

Moments later she replies:

> You put it in your bag. I'm sure you did. Don't
> worry. It's in your emails, too.

Of course it is. Silly me. I can read it on my phone. *Goodness, you must be nervous, Jemima!* I take a large sip of Champagne. Just a little out of practice, that's all. Once I'm there on location, it will all come back to me, I'm sure.

TWENTY-ONE

KIM

OK, Jemima's safely on the plane, and on her way.

I had a moment to myself at last. I took myself down to the basement, to have a quick lie down on the sofa. Sinking onto the sofa, I felt my body relax for the first time in a week.

'Kim? You in there?' George. He must have been right outside the door. He never came down here. I leapt to my feet.

'Hi. Yes. Do you need something, George?' Was I meant to let him in? I stood on my side of the door, he on the other.

'What are you doing in there? I've been looking for you.'

I opened the door, and found him standing there. We looked at each other for a moment. It was the first time that it had been just the two of us in the house alone.

He stepped into the basement, squinting at the lack of light.

'Why are you down here?' I watched him take it all in. My jacket on the arm of the sofa, my bag on the floor.

'I've been sorting out Jemima's old clothes.' He looked around at the bags of clothes that I still needed to sort out. He bent down to look in one bin bag, pulled out a T-shirt, and turned to look at me.

'She's got you doing this?' I nodded.

Then I saw him notice my wash bag on an upturned box. He turned to look at me. 'Have you been staying down here?'

I swallowed. What was I meant to say? I watched him take it all in. The cushions on the sofa that I was using as pillows. The blankets. If he went in the bathroom he would see my towels, my toothbrush.

He turned to look at me. 'Don't you have somewhere else to stay?'

I had to play this very carefully. 'Sometimes it's easier to stay here, if we've had a lot on. Not very often. Just once or twice. Like after Jemima's dinner party.'

'Once or twice...' George looked around, taking it all in. I couldn't read his expression. Concerned? Angry?

He walked back towards the door, then turned to look at me. 'What time is your train?'

'Very early...'

'Oh, poor thing. You have time for a drink, then? I always feel very guilty opening a bottle of wine on my own.'

Dutifully, I followed him upstairs and into the kitchen, where George pulled a bottle of wine out of the dresser, followed by two glasses from the overhead rack.

'It's so quiet when Jemima isn't here.' George smiled and passed me a glass of very dark red wine. 'Try this. I was sent a case from a director I worked with, who has his own vineyard.'

We both took a sip. It was unlike anything I'd tried before. *So this is what expensive wine tastes like?* Of course he knew someone with a vineyard. The Edens really did live in another world. George topped up his glass, then mine. I could see him visibly relax. He was so different when Jemima wasn't around.

'Thank you so much for all you do here. Jemima can be... well, you know. You are very good with her. I appreciate that.' He took another sip. 'She's incredibly excited about this acting job. I do hope it works out for her.'

'It seems like the perfect part for her.'

George nodded enthusiastically. 'Such a good part. It's just, she's... well, you know as well as anyone, she has been through a lot this past few weeks. The rumours, the story. All lies of course. I just hope she manages OK. Being in the spotlight, and this TV series, will bring more attention, and... I do worry.'

George was so kind, he clearly cared for Jemima a lot. Well, they were married. I wondered what Mum would have been like if my dad had stuck around, if she'd had someone to care for her. It was really hard going through life on your own.

'So, tell me about *you*, Kim. I feel we are like ships in the night! You, always running around. Working so hard.'

It was nice, the two of us sitting here. Like it was us that lived here, in this posh house, as if this was our kitchen. The wine was strong – I could feel my body relaxing with each sip.

'Oh, there's nothing much to say, really. Thank you for introducing me to Elle and Leoni. That was really nice of you.'

Leoni had seemed pleased with my new headshots. The new red hair looked great – surely that would help get me some work, make me memorable. I really hope the cost of them would pay off; I tried not to think about that sitting on my credit card. It all seemed unreal – I'd managed to get signed with a top agent, despite not having been to drama school. But hey, why not? She had said I had something different about me. And of course, I knew the Edens.

'Oh, no trouble at all! I remember when I was starting out. It feels good to be paying it forward, you know. Helping someone out.' He smiled at me. 'More wine? It's incredible, isn't it? I must let Tom know.'

I held out my glass. I was in no rush to go and pack. I watched George play with his glass, his hands so large against the delicate stem.

'I have a favour to ask, Kim.' He looked at me, suddenly serious. 'Jemima... she's had so many rejections in the last year or so, and she so badly wants this job to go well. I worry she will put herself under pressure, do you know what I mean?'

So, was this why he had invited me for a glass of wine – to ask a favour.

'I know she seems tough, but really, it's an act. She can be incredibly vulnerable. It's such great news that this job is in Scotland. Relatively close by, but should be nice and quiet for her up there, miles from any press. But still, I do worry. Can you keep an eye on her for me? Let me know how she is?'

Well, that seemed easy enough. I'd be right there with her anyway. 'I think so.' I nodded.

Was he worried about her being harassed by the press? The film set would have proper security and all that, and I wasn't sure I'd be much help regardless. Likely he was worrying too much. Or maybe he didn't trust her now. Did some part of him think that the rumours were true? Looking around the kitchen, it made no sense to me – why would Jemima want to ruin all this?

His whole face crinkled, in that slightly disarming way he had. 'Oh, great, thank you, that is *such* a relief. Just stay close, and if you are worried about her at all, then just call me. If she's struggling at all.'

'Sure. No problem at all.'

'Good!' He picked up the bottle and walked over to the door. 'I'll leave you in peace.'

He paused, and turned to me. 'Oh, and, Kim... Staying here? Let's keep that between us, yes? Our little secret.'

TWENTY-TWO

JEMIMA

Everyone thinks being an actor is so glamorous. And, yes, I guess walking the red carpet and being at parties and things like that do make it look glamorous to outsiders. If you could see me now, standing on this godforsaken windswept coastline, hair whipping about my face! It's freezing here, and there is a light drizzle in the air, which I know will make my hair frizz. But it's so good to get away from home, to have a sense of freedom, of space. There's hardly anyone here – I could be standing at the end of the earth.

OK, I admit that there is something beautiful about the beach, here in St Andrews – such pure white sand and pale blue sea. If it wasn't so cold, it could be a beach in the Caribbean. A pair of students walk along the harbour wall, wrapped in red cloaks, choosing the best place to take photographs of each other. I watch one lean against the ancient stone wall, and her friend steps back, almost to the edge of the harbour. Just one step further and she'll fall into the sea below.

The girls swap places and take more photographs – the blood-red cloaks do look striking against the mossy, damp wall. That red would look really excellent with my hair. I must talk to

wardrobe, and see if there is a scene that would warrant something that colour.

I'm not needed on set until tonight, so I've got time to
explore. If they expect me to sit in that trailer all day, well, that
won't bring out my best side. I'm the only customer at the
toastie shack on the beach. It has a surfboard propped up
outside, which gives it a cheerful vibe, though the barista is
wearing a beanie hat and a yellow padded jacket, and doesn't
look like he wants to get in the sea any time soon. A mac and
cheese toastie? That sounds horrific – for Americans only,
surely. It makes the catering truck food seem sophisticated.
'Black coffee please.' He passes out a paper cup of coffee.

'You here for the filming?'

'Yep.'

'You don't look like a student, so I guessed.' He smiles at me,
thinks he's cute. 'Can you tell me what you're filming?'

'Sorry, no. I'd have to kill you if I told you.'

My phone buzzes. Kim.

> Just arriving in St Andrews. Shall I come to find
> you? Or go to hotel?

I type:

> Come straight to set.

And then I add, 'Thanks'.

The film crew has taken over the small Scottish town, and it
will be easy for Kim to find us. I've walked around most of St
Andrews in about twenty minutes – just three main roads and a
coastal path leading up and over the cliffs. Pretty old stone
buildings, and one massive golf course. They filmed *Chariots of
Fire* on the beach, apparently. Not that I have any plans for
running. I walk back up the hill to where the trailers fill the road
alongside the castle ruins, each parked nose to tail, brash and

white, a stark contrast to the ancient ruins. Orange tape cordons off the area, making it very clear to locals that they're not welcome. Two men in high-vis jackets stand by the path, hired to keep people, and particularly their phones, away from us. Good.

I can only guess at what the TV company have paid to take over this area – must be a fortune. I can hear the beeping of a truck reversing. Scaffolding is being lowered into position in the castle ruins to light tonight's scene.

The young producer is standing next to the catering truck, holding a walkie-talkie and a mug of coffee, iPad rammed under her arm. I plaster on my biggest and most enthusiastic smile.

'Ms Eden! Great, you're here.' She speaks into her handset. 'Jemima Eden's here. OK. Will send her over.'

She clips it onto a strap that cuts across her large chest. 'We were wondering where you'd got to. They're ready for you in hair and make-up.'

This one looks like she could do with a bit of hair and make-up herself. 'I'm not filming 'til tonight. Do I need to do it so soon?'

She looks at me, a little unsure of herself. 'Sorry... just doing what I'm told.'

I stifle a sigh. *OK, play the game, Jemima. Can't be a diva on day one.* 'Of course. Excited to get started! Marianne, isn't it?' *Thank heavens for name badges.*

She nods obediently.

'When my assistant arrives, send her to me, will you?'

TWENTY-THREE

KIM

The train took forever from St Pancras, but the last part of the journey had flown by – the train had hugged the coastline, and I'd stared out of the window the whole way. It was all so beautiful, with beaches and the sea, and tiny boats bobbing in pretty harbours.

A black Land Rover was waiting to collect me from nearby Leuchars train station and we whizzed through country lanes, past actual Highland cows, and under a stone arch into St Andrews. The town was tiny but postcard-perfect, with posh shops lining the street, trees placed symmetrically along the wide pavements, and tables filled with gorgeous people. The driver told me about Prince William and Princess Kate meeting here at university. No, I didn't play golf, but yes, I'd heard it was a big thing here. And suddenly the sea was right there – if we'd driven any further we would have plunged right into it. The town ended on a clifftop, with the towering ruins of a castle right on the edge.

The driver helped me with my bag. 'Caused quite a lot of excitement, you lot being here. Are you an actor?'

I couldn't resist. 'Yes, I am.' OK, I wasn't in this production, but I had an agent, right? Maybe I would be an actor soon.

'I'll look out for you!'

So, this was what it was like to be on a film set! I hauled my bag behind me and walked up to a row of trailers blocking the road. I could see people walking around in black padded coats, talking into handsets, looking very busy and important. A large film camera was being rolled into position. So exciting to be here, to be part of this!

'Closed set. You can't come in.' A large bald man in high-vis looked at me.

'I'm here with Jemima Eden.'

He looked like he didn't believe me. He turned away and spoke into his handset.

A friendly looking woman walked over, iPad in hand.

'You Kim? Hi. I'm Marianne. First Assistant Producer.'

'Hi! Yes, I'm Jemima Eden's PA.'

'She said to expect you. She's in trailer three.' She grinned at me, and nodded towards the far row of trailers. I lifted my bag over thick black cables on the ground and walked past a group of men eating bacon rolls, and made my way towards Jemima's trailer. A woman about my age ran past with a tartan dress, wrapped in plastic.

'Kim! At last.'

Jemima was sitting in front of a mirror, her hair wrapped in an orange towel, while two women applied make-up. I smiled at her reflection.

'Did you print out my script? We can run the lines for tonight's scene.' *Oh god, was I meant to do that?*

'Sorry. I can try and get that sorted for you now.' Surely someone on set had a script printed out? Jemima did not look pleased.

'Can't get the staff these days!' She smiled at the make-up

artists in the mirror. 'Don't worry. You can read it from your phone.'

No 'how was your journey' or 'have you eaten', it was straight to work. I really needed a coffee, but I guessed that this is why I was here, to do Jemima's bidding. *OK, let's do this.* 'Of course! Here it is. From page eight, yes?'

TWENTY-FOUR

JEMIMA

I haven't experienced darkness like this for such a long time. The sky is a rich, inky blackness, covered in stars. It's breathtaking; with no light pollution, the sky is so clear, like it doesn't look real. It reminds me of our bedroom when we were kids. My brother had got us a packet of those plastic stars and planets, and we stuck them on the ceiling with Blu-tac and they glowed in the dark, long after Mum had shouted for us to turn the light out.

'Jemima Eden! So wonderful to meet you.' I recognise that gorgeous Scottish accent from all his film work.

'Donald Scott! How lovely.'

'I was so pleased when they told me you were in this. Playing Vanessa, am I right? We will both be in tonight's scene.'

'How is it going so far?' Donald is playing the main character. He leans in, conspiratorially. 'They are a little amateur, a lot of new kids on the team, but OK. You should see your castle! It will suit you. Lady of the manor.'

I laugh. 'I can't wait.' Donald has the most animated face, so lively and engaging. And those famous brown eyes... This shoot could be a lot of fun.

TWENTY-FIVE

KIM

This was now officially the longest day of my life. I'd been up at five to get the first train here, and then I'd spent the afternoon reading lines with Jemima, and the hours had stretched on and on, and now here we were filming a night scene. But I loved it. The bustle around the film set as actors, directors, camera crew and lighting all got into their positions. Big coats were removed from the stars, and then 'Action!' I wasn't close enough to hear what Jemima and her co-stars were saying, but I could just about see her, acting her scene. And of course, I knew the script off by heart.

And then, 'Cut!' The director – a tall, white man in a beanie hat – would talk to the actors, and then they would do it all again. A light rain shower at one point halted filming, while assistants ran around getting coats and huge golf umbrellas to shelter the actors. Hair and make-up came sweeping in, worked their magic, and then it was all go again. 'Silence on set!' We all stood there dutifully, not daring to move or make a sound in case we ruined anything. I'd followed Jemima onto the set when she was called, just in case she needed me, and that seemed to be the right thing to do, as she popped over to me a few times, to get water, or to run a line again. It really didn't look that difficult being an actor, especially when you knew how much she was getting paid.

It really was magical here, with the moonlight reflecting across the sea. Maybe one day it would be me acting in a scene, with people running around after me. I was so close, I could taste it. I could visualise myself standing there, dressed in a long tweed coat, with a fur collar, like Jemima. Her red lips were visible from here, lit by an overhead light, casting a soft light on her. She looked so happy, confident, sharing a joke with Donald Scott, as they waited for the director to check the film. Then it was 'Cut!' again, and everyone burst into life around me.

Jemima walked over to me, an assistant holding an umbrella over her head.

'Kim. Can you go to my trailer? Get me my pills. The ones in the white tin.'

Pills? I nodded. 'Sure. Anything else?'

She looked at me, impatient. 'No. Quick, please. I've got a migraine coming on.'

'Can I help you with anything, Ms Eden?' Marianne, the nice assistant producer, appeared beside us.

'No. Kim can help me.'

'OK. We do have runners if you need anything. We will stop for a break soon. Get some hot drinks for everyone.' She clearly wanted Jemima back in position.

I smiled at them both. 'It's not a problem. Back soon.'

Jemima's trailer was a mess inside, and I picked up her jumper, folding it neatly. I looked around; she hadn't said where her pills would be. I went into the tiny bathroom, with a basin tucked in the corner, a narrow shelf, but no medicines in there. Jemima's handbag sat on the table by the window. It felt weird looking through her stuff, but she had sent me here, hadn't she? I looked inside. A kindle, a magazine, a Chanel compact, a packet of sweets. My mum used to have a little compact like this. Hers wasn't Chanel though. I slid it out of its lovely black velvet pouch and clicked it open. I looked at my face in the tiny mirror. My eyes looked uneven and there was acne developing on my chin. So pale. Why had I been born so odd-looking? Nothing at all like my mum. She had a lovely face. Rounder, prettier. People never thought we looked alike. I took the tiny flat sponge and lightly dabbed the compressed powder, then wiped it across my nose. So soft! My skin instantly looked clearer, less shiny. I snapped it shut, and put it back in the bag.

Some keys, two credit cards, tissues, and a small tin. I prised it open, and inside, pills. Mostly white and round, a few blue, shaped like lozenges. *What are all these for, Jemima?* How interesting. I put the tin in my pocket. I felt quite important making my way across the set.

'Here you go.' I passed Jemima the tin and a bottle of water.

'Thanks.' She turned her back on me, and I went back to stand at the sidelines.

I crawled into bed that night, exhausted. Lying there, I tried to take it all in. It was a huge crew and team working on the film. Most of them were also staying in this hotel overlooking the golf course. I wondered if I would get to know more people tomorrow, get to network, maybe even meet the director himself. They'd all think of me as Jemima's assistant, of course, but I could slip in that I was also an actor, maybe get some email addresses at the end of all this, send them my new Spotlight link. It was so worth being here! Where it was all happening. This was exactly where I needed to be.

I was up early, full of excitement for what the day ahead would bring. I helped myself to a plate of scrambled eggs and walked over to an empty table in the window. So much choice for breakfast – I could really get used to this lifestyle! I could see Marianne and some of the crew sat at the large round table in the centre of the room, but no one looked up as I walked past, so I didn't try and sit with them. A waiter in a tartan waistcoat offered me coffee in a soft Scottish accent. So nice to have someone looking after me for a change.

My phone buzzed. I answered it quickly, to not annoy the other people in the room.

'Kim? Hi. You got there OK?' *George.* He was calling early.

'Yes thanks. Long train journey, but made it.'

'Great! How is everything going? Having fun?'

'All good. Not sure Jemima is up yet. I haven't seen her.'

'I've tried her a few times. I was beginning to think the signal wasn't working up there! But here you are. So phones work just fine, north of the border.'

'They were filming 'til nearly two last night. I'm sure she'll call you back when she gets a chance.'

'Oh, for sure! I know what those film sets can be like. Long days, late nights.'

Across the room, I heard a familiar laugh, loud voices, very jolly for this time in the morning. I turned to look. Jemima had walked in with Donald Scott. The pair caused quite a stir, heads turning, as crew and other hotel guests turned to watch these two beautiful, well-known faces enter the room. Jemima looked lovely, in her grey cashmere sweater and skinny jeans.

'You still there, Kim?' George said in my ear.

'Yes, sorry. A waiter was talking to me,' I lied. I watched Donald place his hand on Jemima's back, and show her to a table near the fireplace.

'OK. Have a good day. Tell Jemima I was asking after her.'

George hung up.

TWENTY-SIX

JEMIMA

I barely slept last night. The lines I'd messed up kept going round and round in my head. The way the director had looked at me, like I was a complete idiot... I couldn't get that look out of my mind. We'd had to do the scene so many times, and it was made very clear it was my fault. Donald got it right, every time, and he had more lines! It was me that couldn't get it right. The lights shining in my face hadn't helped, it was so distracting. And so many faces watching me, all standing there, staring. Waiting for me to get it right so they could all call it a night and get to their hotel rooms. I could see it on that Marianne's face – they'd all decided that I was going to be the difficult one. At least the pills had helped to calm my nerves.

It had been past two when I finally got into bed. I could tell the scene hadn't gone the way Frank had wanted, and it was meant to be an easy one! Tomorrow was going to be in the castle, and there would be so many of us – the whole cast, plus extras. If I couldn't get my lines right, it would be so humiliating.

I bumped into Donald on the way down to breakfast. He looked annoyingly refreshed. I put on my best smile and joined him in the dining room. Everyone turned as we walked in. Why hadn't the production company booked somewhere more private? The room seemed to be full of tourists, here to play golf, I guess, all delighted to see some actors here. Something to talk about when they returned to their dull lives back home. I saw Kim make her way over.

'Morning, Ms Eden. I'll be in the lobby if you need anything.'

Goodness, how formal of her – showing off for the others, no doubt. I smile at Donald. 'My assistant, Kim. An actor herself, when not working for me.'

Donald leaps up, rather theatrically I think, and shakes Kim's hand. She looks a little startled. 'Always lovely to meet a fellow actor.'

Kim nods, and scuttles away.

'You brought your assistant with you? That's very showbiz, Jemima.' Donald smiles, as he pours himself another cup of coffee. The waiter practically runs over to give him a fresh pot. Donald rewards him with a dazzling glimpse of his perfect teeth.

'Jealous? Don't you have an assistant?'

He laughs. 'My life probably isn't as complicated as yours.'

What does he mean by that? I watch him bite into his avocado toast. Not exactly a traditional Scottish breakfast. He's read the stories about me, then.

'That was all made-up. You know what the press are like.'

He glances up at me. 'Shame. I was rather hoping you made a habit of it.'

I can't help smiling at that. 'You're married, Donald.'

'So are you.' He grins, a little too sure of himself for my liking. 'Most of the crew will be talking about us, anyway. So why not enjoy ourselves, when so far away from home?'

Was he for real? 'It's Scotland, Donald, not the ends of the earth.' I glance around the room. People are pretending not to be watching us, but I can feel their eyes on us. It takes just one of these people to post something on social media, or call a newspaper, try and sell a story. I'll have breakfast delivered to my room tomorrow.

I get up, appetite gone. 'I'll see you on set. Enjoy your breakfast.'

TWENTY-SEVEN

KIM

I should have packed warmer clothes. Although the sky was a perfect cloudless blue, it was freezing as soon as you stepped outside.

'Morning!' Marianne walked across the crunchy gravel towards me, looking very wide awake.

'Hi! You staying here, too?'

'No such luck. We're in the hotel down the road. I was kept awake by clanking pipes all last night. You're here though?'

'Yes, it's really posh.'

'Wow. Jemima must have organised that for you.'

'I guess she wants me close by in case she needs me.'

Marianne nodded. She was wearing a thick orange jumper that really didn't flatter her rosy face. It did look warm and comfy though. Maybe I could have a look round some charity shops and find something warmer – a thicker coat. If it was a late night again, I'd freeze in this.

'We'll need Jemima on set at noon. You going to be there?' Marianne asked.

'Yes, if she wants me to. I'm not sure if—'

'It must be so strange being a PA to Jemima Eden. What do you do all day?'

'Probably same as you. Run around, organise things when needed.'

Marianne laughed at that. 'Sounds about right. I wouldn't go back to being an actor. Too stressful. This suits me much better. I hated not knowing when I would work.'

'I know exactly what you mean. It's so unpredictable.'

'You're an actor? I went to Bristol Old Vic. Years ago now.'

I didn't feel the need to correct her. *Flatter her instead*, I thought. 'That's so cool. I wish I'd gone to somewhere like that.' That much was true.

Marianne's handset buzzed. 'No rest for the wicked! See you later. Kim, isn't it? The crew will try and get a drink tonight, if you want to come? As long as Jemima gets her lines right, and we aren't all there past midnight again!'

TWENTY-EIGHT

JEMIMA

This is why I do it, isn't it? To act, to perform, to share stories. But this is nothing like acting on a stage, where you get the audience reaction straight away. You know if they love you – you get to hear the laughs, see the smiles, watch the standing ovation. Here, on a film set, the only way you know if you've done a good job is if the director tells you. It's all down to one person – usually a man, let's be honest. He watches you, then goes off to look at his monitor, and then decides if you are good enough, or not.

Frank just stands there, arms folded, watching. His assistants run around putting us in position, telling lighting what to do, checking in with Frank, and then we get the signal, and we do the scene again. And again, until Frank is happy.

At least we're indoors tonight – just as well as the rain is sheeting down outside. With a real fire in the vast stone fireplace, spotlights shining down on us, and my thick tweed costume, I'm starting to melt. Why don't wardrobe think of these things when they design costumes? My hair is piled up, and a very fake-looking hairpiece pinned to my scalp. God, I want to rip it off. Donald, by contrast, looks cool and relaxed, as ever.

We've done our first scene, where we walk down the stair-case into the hallway. I have to say, I did feel a little excited when I first arrived at the castle. Such large rooms, high ceilings, and the most beautiful stained-glass windows – by the artist Charles Rennie Mackintosh, apparently. The bleak grey stone exterior didn't give any clues to how lovely it is inside.

My mood has deflated quickly though. When we arrived, Marianne took Donald and I into a side room, which really, could have been a room in my house, it was so normal. Standing there, either side of the fireplace, were the two real owners of the house. He was short and balding. She was willowy, posh-looking, wearing a striped shirt and a thin, padded gilet. The American accent surprised me as she stepped forward to intro-duce herself.

'Michelle Campbell. So pleased to meet you! Welcome to our home.'

I couldn't fail to notice the enormous diamond on her left hand.

'So exciting to be here,' I managed.

'So formal!' Donald stepped forward, and kissed Michelle on both cheeks, making her giggle. Her husband looked at me, as if expecting the same. *Not a chance.*

'Lord and Lady Campbell have been so generous letting us film in their home. It really is an honour. Please know that we are going to take such good care of your castle.' *Steady on, Marianne, you are gushing.* I had no doubt that Lord and Lady Campbell were being paid very well to rent out their home for the film. So, we'd been pulled in here, because, I guess, the Campbells had asked to meet some stars of the film.

'Glenacre is a baronial mansion, really. We don't tend to use the word *castle*,' Lord Campbell felt the need to say. I looked at him. I felt sure Michelle knew all about the 'baronial mansion' before she married him.

'Well, it's lovely. And it's so lovely to meet you both.' I glanced at Marianne. How long were we meant to stand here?

Michelle looked at her husband. 'We were hoping to meet Katherine Roberts? Is she filming today?'

'She's in tonight's scene. Everyone is. It's the big scene that actually ends the film, but we are filming it right at the start, while we are all up here.'

'Will we get to meet her? Jeremy is a huge fan.' Michelle beamed at her husband.

Oh, so we were not quite the stars they were hoping for. 'Marianne, I think we need to...' I turned to head towards the door. Donald had better follow me.

'Of course! Filming awaits!'

'For god's sake. That was embarrassing,' I whispered to Donald as we walked through the hallway.

'All part of the game, Jemima. See you on set later.'

I've never worked with Katherine Roberts, but I know a lot about her. Younger than me, she's already won two BAFTAs and been nominated for an Oscar for a tedious film about a ballet dancer who loses her leg in a car accident. She walks onto the set, looking like she owns the place. Tall, long neck, freakishly large eyes, she really only could have been an actor in life – that or a trophy wife. How come she gets to wear a beautiful silver evening dress, and I have to wear tweed? She swishes across the room, past the admiring glances of the crew lining the walls, and arrives in front of me.

'Jemima Eden! So lovely to meet you at last!' She performs an air kiss, leaving plenty of space between us, then beams at me. She has the most enormous mouth.

'Katherine! Isn't this fun? What a place to work in. I've

wanted to collaborate with you for so long. It's great to finally have the chance.' I really am a good actor.

'Me too. And here's Donald! Darling!' She turns to embrace Donald, who has appeared by her side. 'Look at you! So Scottish-looking.'

Donald laughs, and swirls his kilt for her benefit. Behind him, I can see the extras starting to file into the hall, all in various evening outfits, the men in kilts, the women in evening dresses, tartan sashes in place to remind the audience that we are very much in Scotland. God, I hope this film isn't going to be terrible.

'Places, everyone, please!' Marianne shouts across the room, and a small army of people in black move around, showing us all where to stand.

Showtime.

TWENTY-NINE

KIM

It was fun watching Jemima in action. If I stood in the corridor off the main hall, no one noticed me, and when the director, Frank, started the scene, I could stand just behind a camera operator and watch. Her face changed when acting. So animated and happy. Then, 'Cut!' and her expression returned to its usual resting bitch face. It was interesting to watch – on and off. I could do that. Smile, and be the perfect host of the party, and then relax, be back here in reality. My only job seemed to be to hold her script, just in case she needed to come over and check the lines, but so far, so good. I had a bag with water, pills and phone in it, just in case. When they finished that take, I stepped back into the corridor, and took the moment to text George:

> We are filming in a castle! Jemima doing well.

Bouncing dots, and then he replied. That was fast.

> Great! If you get a chance, send pics!!

I was pretty sure that would not be allowed. Could you

imagine if I took a picture on my phone and someone noticed? What if the flash went off?

I walked over to the table where someone had set up a coffee urn.

'Hey, how's it going?' Marianne appeared next to me.

'OK. You?'

She let out a huge sigh. 'Exhausting! I have not sat down for hours. My feet are in shock.'

'You do seem busy.'

'Constant! The food stylists are complaining about the lack of space to set up the banquet scene. Some of the extras are moaning about their shoes. Not the right sizes. I mean, they are only wearing them for a couple of hours. And don't get me started on Katherine. Oh my god, I need a drink. Something stronger than coffee.'

'Yeah, me too.' I had found that agreeing with people was a quick way to make them like you.

She looked at me. 'Is Jemima being a pain? I sympathise. Give me your number and I'll text you where the crew are meeting tonight. Leon knows a bar that does a late lock-in.' She grinned. 'Catch you later.'

Two takes later, and just one visit from Jemima to check her phone, and I was free to join the queue outside for the catering truck. Someone had set up gazebos to shelter us from the rain, and we huddled underneath, waiting our turn. Two men in high-vis jackets waited next to me, not speaking. I tried to talk, to pass the time.

'I bet the actors don't have to queue out in the rain.'

One nodded. 'They have a marquee out the back.'

Of course. That must be where Jemima was. I could see people collecting their steaming bowls of food, and then dart back under the gazebos, where they stood, sheltering from the rain that was making its way in sideways. I had a better idea. I walked round the edge of the building, gravel crunching, rain hitting the ground all around me, until I found the marquee. The security guard was on his phone, so I walked in, confidently. He barely glanced at me. Really, anyone could have got in.

'Kim! There you are.' Jemima was sat a trestle table, a huge black coat covering her costume. Her make-up looked pretty hideous in this light. Yellowish skin, dark red lips. I guess it looked OK on film. Somehow, they had made the marquee cosy and warm, with sheepskins covering the benches, and dried thistles and heather on the tables.

On the far side of the tent, chefs doled out plates of salmon, vegetables and steaks, from large silver containers. *How the other half live.*

'How's it going?' I asked, hovering at her side.

Jemima speared a tiny piece of broccoli into her mouth.

'I've got the dinner scene next. With Katherine.' She looked at me, and I was surprised to see that she looked a little nervous.

'Oh, that scene! You are great in that.' We'd gone over the lines for that a few times before we left for Scotland. And she had known it, most of the time.

'Thanks. I'm running the words in my head, but they are starting to blur a little. It's different now I'm here.' She glanced around the room. On the next table, Katherine Roberts was sitting very close to Donald Scott. Across from them were the two actors playing the brothers. We knew one of them was going to kill Katherine at the end of the film, but of course, here, it was all fun and getting along. I wondered why Jemima hadn't sat with them.

'We can run the lines now, if you like?'

Her face brightened at that. 'Can we? I think I have time.' She glanced across at the other actors. 'I'm not in the next scene. Shall we find a quiet place?'

I looked at the food. That salmon looked really good. Jemima stared at me, expectantly.

'Um... sure. Whatever you need.'

'Great! We can go to my trailer.'

As we emerged from the marquee, a young woman appeared with a giant golf umbrella and held it over Jemima's head. Not mine, I noticed. We walked in an awkward huddle to the trailer, and climbed in.

'I can't concentrate, can't get a moment to myself to relax. I feel like I'm permanently on show.' She tugged at her hairpiece trying to make it a little more comfortable. It did look very tight.

'Can I get you a drink?' I offered.

'There's wine in the fridge.' She indicted to a small brown cupboard under the sink. 'Glasses up there.'

I didn't think wine would help with the line situation, but I was sure my opinion wouldn't be welcome. I poured two glasses of wine and sat across from Jemima. She turned her head slightly, but I saw her take a pill with a large swig of wine.

'Don't judge, Kim. It helps my anxiety.' *Oh, right. So not for headaches, then.*

I opened the script at the dinner scene. 'It's not all about the money. You should know that.' I said, and looked at Jemima, waiting for her line.

'Only a rich man could ever say that,' she replied. A bit flat, but, hey, it was only a run-through.

'So, what drives you, Vanessa? Don't say family.'

'Family is everything to me. Everyone knows that. Oh, fuck. That's not the line... what is it, Kim?'

'Family is everything to me. My life... All I ever wanted was children.'

'That's such a stupid line. She would never say that. It's out of character.' Jemima leaned back onto the cushions. 'That's why it won't go in. It doesn't make sense.'

I wanted to say, 'You've had this script for ages. You had this script when you agreed to do this film. You have no idea how lucky you are to be here, doing this. How privileged you are, to get this opportunity. So many actors would kill for this chance, to be here, doing your role. I could do this role. You just have to put the work in and learn the lines. You have no idea what I would do, to be in your position...' But I didn't say any of that out loud, of course.

'Let's start from the top of the scene again. You've got this. You're so good! It will make perfect sense when you are there, in position, with the other actors. The lines will come to you. Let's run it through again.'

Jemima looked at me nodding. 'Kim. You are *such* a help. I am so lucky to have you. OK, you start.'

Jemima got through her scene, and everyone was relieved when Frank finally shouted 'Cut!' for the last time.

I watched the camera and lighting crew start to roll up leads, and turn off lights. I walked over to where Jemima was chatting with a couple of the actors, to see if she needed me for anything. Just as I reached her, she turned pointedly away from me. I watched them all walk together into the green room. Not so much as a 'good night'.

OK, well, that suited me. Marianne had texted me the pub name earlier. The Saint was on the main road in St Andrews, and was heaving when I arrived, although it was surely close to closing time. I recognised a man waiting at the bar – one of the sound crew.

'We're downstairs,' he said, edging past me, holding three sloppy pints of beer.

I ordered a beer, to fit in, then followed him down the stairs. The noise hit me – the room was rammed with people, all talking at once, and The Killers, loud, coming from a DJ in the corner. Gone were the padded black coats and high-vis jackets, instead, everyone looked so colourful and creative, more animated, laughing.

'Kim! You made it!' Marianne pushed her way through the crowd. She was wearing a yellow-and-orange sleeveless dress, which showed off amazing tattoos, snaking up her arms and across her chest.

'Thanks for inviting me.'

'Well, you're one of us really. Not one of them. You got a drink? Good. Come on, let me introduce you to people.'

She made space for me at a large, crowded table. 'This is Kim. Works for Jemima.'

This got a few theatrical 'ooohs', followed by laughs.

'I'm Steph. I do hair and make-up. I've done Jemima's.' I recognised her, said hi. Steph looked really different dressed up for a night out, so glamorous.

'Do you all know each other?' I asked Steph.

'Most of us, yes. I trained with Adam. He worked with Dave at the BBC. I've worked with Marianne before. Once you get in with a production company, they keep getting you back. As long as you're not obnoxious, of course.'

More beers appeared, and Marianne waved a credit card at the bartender. 'Frank is paying!' The stories flowed. Steph used to be married to the head of security, who no one seemed to like, and there was a lot of discussion about one of the camera operators having a massive crush on Katherine. 'Like she is ever going to talk to you!'

A wooden board of bread, hummus and olives appeared, and I ate a few strips of pitta. My head was starting to swim from all the alcohol.

'So, what's she like? *Jemima.*' Marianne was smiling at me, her face round and shiny.

'OK. You know, she's my boss. Tells me what to do.'

'Did she really sleep with that guy?' Steph leaned across and asked.

'Rory Jackson!' Marianne added. 'I worked with him ages ago. On *Dragonslayer*. He was amazing.'

'Can't blame her, if she did sleep with him. He's hot,' Steph added. 'They're all at it.'

'I don't think so,' I interjected. 'Her husband would be furious if she had. And he seems pretty chilled about it.' As I said the words, I realised that was true, despite my own misgivings.

Jemima couldn't have slept with Rory, or if she had, she had somehow totally convinced George that the rumours weren't true. He had been so caring about her, and I didn't see him as the type to put up with an affair.

'So much of what you read is made-up. The papers just make stuff up now, for clickbait. He and Jemima do know each other though – he came to the house.'

They were all listening to me, as if I was suddenly the expert on these matters. 'I have to look after Jemima's social media, and you wouldn't believe the shit that people say to her on there. It's so toxic.'

Marianne nodded. 'I worked with an actress who nearly killed herself 'cos of what people said about her. It was so sad. She got so much grief online. Mind you, she was a bit unsteady to start with. No idea why she wanted to be an actress.'

I took a sip of my beer. 'I'm an actor.' I told the table. 'But it's really tough. I have tried to get acting work... I just got a new agent, but well, here I am. Working for Jemima.'

'It's *so* hard trying to make it as an actor. Will over there went to drama school. He's a producer now, which is pretty good though. Are you, like, a PA?' Steph asked. 'We weren't exactly sure what you were doing for Jemima.' A few of them laughed. 'That sounded weird, didn't mean it to, sorry.'

'There's more to do when we're at home. Appointments, dealing with her admin, running her household, that sort of thing. I'm not that busy up here.'

'Sounds cushy to me. Nice work if you can get it.'

I laughed. Yes, it did sound OK. And it had brought me here, to this place, with these amazing people. I looked around the table, at the smiling faces, who had so effortlessly welcomed me into their group. *So, this is what it's like to have friends.* I liked the feeling.

THIRTY

JEMIMA

Two missed calls from George. I text him to say I've just got back to my room and need a bath, and I'll call him in the morning.

Just as I sink into the hot, bubbly water, the phone rings. I feel the water start to relax my aching body, my sore muscles. I can see the bruise on my arm was starting to heal and fade. *Ignore it, Jem.* The phone rings again. *Oh god, it might be Frank, or one of the producers. Maybe they need to tell me something ahead of filming tomorrow?*

Reluctantly, I climb out of the bath, and wrap myself in a large towel.

George. I swallow. I could cut him off, but he'll just keep ringing.

'Hi, darling. I was trying you earlier. You must have finished ages ago.'

'Just got back. The castle is outside St Andrews. I was in the bath.'

He ignores that. 'How are you getting on? Are you getting your lines right?'

'Mostly.'

'You know how film crews hate actors who can't get the lines. What's Katherine like? As good as everyone says?'

'She's great. Nice, actually. We get on well.' Katherine has been word-perfect, of course.

'Oh, that's so great. It's so important to get on with your co-stars. Sets the tone of the whole set.' *I know that, George.* OK, it has been a while since I've been in a film, but I'm not totally hopeless.

'And Donald? What's he like?' *Ah, so is this why George is calling me?* I pull my towel tighter around me.

'He's very good. Professional. We had to do our scene a few times, but he seemed completely unfazed by that.'

Silence from George, and then, 'A few times. OK. I am sure you will get into the swing of it. You just need to show them what a pro you are.'

But I am showing them what a pro I am. I did my scenes really well, and was calm with everyone. We'd been on set for hours and I hadn't once complained about that stupid hairpiece, that was pinned far too tightly to my scalp. I really should have complained to Frank about that. It was hard to concentrate with a tension headache.

'What time are you on set tomorrow?' George is still talking.

'They are picking me up at eight. A scene on the beach.'

'Wow, so glamorous! Maybe run the lines again before you sleep. Apparently they settle into the brain that way.'

'OK.'

'And don't forget. You don't have to do this. You can always come home. Any time you want.'

And let everyone down? There's no way I'm doing that.

George hangs up at last. It's almost midnight and my body aches from standing on set all day in that stiff costume, but the bathwater has got cold. George is right – I need to be good, especially if I'm acting alongside Katherine, who everyone clearly adores. I pull out my script, and turn to tomorrow's scene. I reach for my pills – they will help me to concentrate.

THIRTY-ONE

KIM

Jemima looked exhausted as she got into the car, and barely spoke to me on the drive to set. We were dropped off at the trailer and Jemima thanked the driver profusely, and then shut the door with a loud sigh.

'Kim, can you run into town? Get me something for my throat. I don't want to bother the runners. Last thing I need is a rumour that I'm not feeling well.'

'Of course.'

Outside, I could see some of the crew from last night, waiting for breakfast by the catering truck. I waved. It would be so nice to go and hang out with them for a while, have a coffee, but no, I had to look after Mrs Eden.

It was a beautiful day out here, the small town coming alive. I bought throat medicine, like a good PA, and headed back to Jemima. On my left, the sea sparkled, and looked so inviting, but I knew it would be icy cold. It would be a gorgeous morning for a walk along the white sandy beach. I could ask Jemima if I could head out for an hour; maybe there would be time before filming started? Me and Mum loved going to the beach, though it was a train ride to the nearest one, and pebbly when you got there. We loved it anyway though, paddling, getting fish and chips, lying there, getting sunburned faces. It would do Jemima good to get out of the trailer, maybe get some sea air herself. She was probably more used to places like the Caribbean, warm water and sunshine, that sort of thing.

'Hi, I'm back,' I called out as I stepped inside.

Jemima looked up at me, phone in hand, momentarily thrown. 'I'll call you back.'

'Sorry. Here you go.' I handed over the packet of pills.

'Kim. I was on the phone,' she snapped.

'Sorry.' My happy mood was gone in an instant.

'Get me a glass of water. Honestly, Kim. Knock next time.'

I passed her the glass of water, and watched her take some pills, and then open the packet of throat lozenges.

'Can you give me some space? Come back in an hour or so?'

Maybe she needed a nap – she didn't look herself at all.

'Sure. See you later.'

THIRTY-TWO

JEMIMA

When I see it's Rory calling, my mood improves instantly. He hasn't called since the story came out, not wanting to create any more problems for me, probably.

'Jemima! This has all been such a bloody nightmare. How are you getting on?

'I'm OK. Just started a short filming job.'

'Well done, you. Oh god, Jemima, I am getting so much shit here. The press were camped outside the house for days!'

'Tell me about it.' I've been through the same, he does know that, right? 'Rory. I'm so glad you called. The filming is so intense. I'm up in Scotland. Have you worked with Frank Delaney before? He's such a tough taskmaster—'

'Frank? Oh, he's fine. Lucky you getting to escape up to Scotland.'

'I guess so. It does feel far away. No press bothering me here.'

'Glad to hear it. So... what does George think about it all?'

Since when does he care about George's opinion? 'He's fine. Doesn't believe the stories. Thinks you made it up.'

'Really... that's not the impression I get. He left a foul message on my phone. God knows how he got my number.'

George hasn't mentioned that to me. I've told him it was all lies, rumours, because Rory had been at our house for dinner. George had had his fair share of press intrusion over the years – he knows the game. PR love a gossipy love story, especially when they have a film to promote.

'Listen, Jemima. Let's leave it a while. That OK with you? I don't think either of us want any more hassle.'

I feel my skin go cold. The thought of not seeing Rory for ages. I think back to when we met. We were working together on a small regional play, before either of us were famous. We were so similar, Rory and I. We'd hang out between rehearsals, laughing, sharing stories of the terrible jobs we'd had, the people we'd met, the crazy directors we'd had to deal with. Me and him have something special. We're a partnership, see the world in the same way.

'Jemima, you there? You're very quiet.'

'Is this about George calling you? Has he told you to stop seeing me?'

'It's not him as such... I don't want any grief for you either.'

'This is crazy. I am up here for another week or so, and then let's meet up when I'm back.'

'No, Jemima. Listen. It's best that we don't see each other.'

'So, this *is* about George. Are you *scared* of him?'

'He knows a lot of people in this business.'

'Oh my god, Rory. I can't believe you said that...'

The door opens, and Kim appears, looking very pleased with herself. *Perfect timing...*

I cut Rory dead.

THIRTY-THREE

KIM

'I've been looking for you! There you are.' Marianne came puffing towards me on the beach. Break over. There must be some issue with Jemima that needed smoothing over. I reached in my bag for my phone. No missed calls.

'You're needed on set.' Marianne stopped next to me, taking a deep breath. 'Wow, it is so beautiful here!' I followed her gaze out to sea. The aquamarine sea, gently lapped on the shore. It really was gorgeous. I stood up, ready to leave this tranquil space and head back to Jemima. I hoped she was in a better mood. Marianne walked alongside me.

'So, I've got some very cool news. You're an actor, right? Well, we need you on set.'

'To do what?' I looked at her, confused.

'Stand in. Do some acting. We'd cast a student, but she has just told us she doesn't have the right to work here. She's from the US. *Now* she tells us. A right mess. We did days of castings. Frank is furious with the casting director. And then I said, what about Kim?' She looked so pleased with herself.

'You want me to be in the film?' I couldn't take it in. 'To do what?'

'It's a tiny part. Only one line, but you're the right age, and I'm sure you can do it.'

'That's amazing! Thank you so much!' I grabbed her, and pulled her into a tight hug. 'Are you sure? Don't I have to ask my agent, or something?'

My mind was whirring with so many questions. I needed to call Leoni, check that it was OK. Surely she would be pleased, right? Would I get paid? Or was it just a small walk-on part, like an extra, and maybe I just got expenses or something? I'd do it, anyway, to help Marianne, but if I got paid, that would be amazing.

'Oh, and I need to check in with Jemima.'

'Oh, yes. You better had. It's only a few hours of filming, so it really shouldn't be an issue. Tell her it would really help Frank. You need to come and meet him. Come on.' Marianne started to walk up the beach.

I thought of Jemima, sitting in her trailer. How would she take this news? I hoped she would be happy for me. I knew George would be.

'I'll go and tell Jemima, then come and find you.'

You know what, if Jemima said no, I would do it anyway. This is what I wanted to do – act, not hang around being an assistant. She could fire me if she wanted, I didn't care. Once the director had seen me acting, he might want to cast me again. This was my chance.

I ran a little, caught up with Marianne, and pulled her into another hug. 'You're a star. Thank you so much. I really owe you!'

THIRTY-FOUR

JEMIMA

What the actual fuck? Frank wants Kim to be in the film? She burst into my trailer, looking like an excited puppy. Is he trying to wind me up? She's here as *my* assistant. I have an important scene this evening and I need her to help me run the lines.

'It's not convenient. And also, Kim, unprofessional. You work for *me*.'

God, she looked so desperate for my approval.

'It's just one scene.'

I try to compose myself.

'Frank asked for you? For you specifically?' This has all come out of the blue. Why hasn't he spoken to me about it first?

'Marianne suggested me. They had a problem... a work visa problem. I'd be filling in for another actor. It's only a small part, Jemima.'

When did she started addressing me by my first name? It used to be Mrs Eden. Marianne... I'll remember that. I can see Kim pulling at the bottom of her jumper, trying to stay calm. She does remind me of myself at that age. So eager, so desperate to work. The red hair is starting to grow out and you can make out her roots. I could say no, of course. But if I say no, I'll look like the bad guy here. And I'll be doing Frank a favour, so that is a good thing. I turn on a smile. 'Actually... I think it's wonderful news, Kim. Well done, you! I can't wait to see what you do.'

'Thank you!' She practically runs out of the trailer.

I look out of the window and watch her run across the parking lot. She got an agent, because of me. And now this acting job. Resourceful girl. I'll have to watch this one.

THIRTY-FIVE

KIM

Being surrounded by cameras on a film set felt amazing! To be among all these famous actors, hair and make-up done, and in a costume, waiting to say my lines, was like a dream come true.

Over to my right, I could see Jemima and Donald waiting to enter, to do their scene. OK, mine was a really small part compared to theirs, but it was a start. I was playing the nanny, and was in a grey dress and white apron, so not glamorous but I didn't care. My shoes were a little tight, clearly meant for the girl who dropped out, but that was OK, I could handle it for a few hours.

And then I was on. I had to enter, say my line, 'The children are ready,' and nod. That was it, but I loved it!

I'd only had to do my scene twice, which was great that I got it right so quickly, but also a shame, as I would have done it a hundred times if they had asked. Right then, I knew, this was what I wanted to do. I could hardly believe people got paid to act, it was so much fun!

'Cut! Excellent. Clear the set please,' Frank called out from between the cameras.

'Great job!' Marianne was standing by the edge of the set, clipboard in hand.

'Thank you so much! I loved it.'

'Wardrobe please, Miss Conner.' A woman I recognised from the pub indicated for me to follow her. I would be sad to remove my costume and get back to reality.

'Kim. One moment.'

To my surprise, Frank, the director, was walking towards *me*. 'Great job. And thank you for helping us out at very short notice.' Marianne was nodding enthusiastically at Frank.

'I was so pleased to be asked.' I couldn't believe he was talking to me!

'Jemima's assistant, right? And you're with the Elle Lobina Agency?'

I nodded.

'Excellent. So I know where to find you. I have another project coming up. You might be right for the daughter.' He smiled at me and turned to Marianne. 'Can you make sure I have Kim's details?'

Had that just happened? Frank Delaney had spoken to me. And he might have more work for me? This was all working out better than I could ever have imagined.

'Come on, you. You need to get that costume back.' Marianne leaned in and whispered, 'You smashed it.'

THIRTY-SIX

JEMIMA

Frank is being a complete dick. There was nothing wrong with that take. My lines were flawless, and I did exactly as he asked. Donald was slightly off, stepped back too far on the second take, and I had to lean into him, and now that's *my* fault, apparently.

'Jemima. This scene is more subtle. It's a moment of sharing information. They are pleased with themselves, yes, but not conspirators.' What is Frank moaning about? Donald raises his eyebrows at me.

'Go again.'

So I tone it down, but that isn't good enough either, too quiet. Exasperated, I let out a long exhale. I swear I see the cameramen exchange glances. *Well, you try it, if you think you can do better.*

This dress is ridiculously hot under the lights. Where's Kim? I could do with a glass of water. No sight of her. I called over to one of the runners, who looks terrified. For goodness' sake, it's not that hard to find water.

'OK, ready, Jemima. Let's get it right this time.'

Like it's all my fault!

. . .

I'm exhausted when I get back to my hotel room, and throw myself on the bed. I called Elle. It takes far too long for her to pick up.

'Jemima. Is everything alright?'

'No, not really Elle. Frank has been obnoxious all day. He wants us back in tomorrow. I thought I'd have finished by now.' The bedside clock glows 23.30 at me. Has she been in bed? It's a Saturday, so not that late, really, for a weekend.

A pause at the end of the line. 'That does sound tough. Must have been a very long day.'

I feel slightly deflated. 'Yes, it was. Can you check in with him tomorrow, find out how much longer I will be needed?' I feel the need to take back some control on this.

'I will. No problem. Frank did message to say that Kim had done a terrific job. I'm so pleased for her.'

'Did he? Did he say anything about me then?'

Elle pauses. 'Not on that call. It was earlier today.' Elle sounds flustered. Most unlike her. 'It's lovely, isn't it? Helping these newcomers into the business.'

I nod. I'd watched Kim do her tiny part, playing the nanny. To be honest, it's the sort of part that might get cut in the edit.

'It's late, Jemima, darling. Well done for today. I'll check in with Frank for you, and call tomorrow. I'm sure you were brilliant. You get some rest.'

I lay there for a while, too wired to go to sleep. Elle works for me. Not Kim. If Frank wants to talk about anyone, it should be me.

THIRTY-SEVEN

KIM

I felt really sad to leave St Andrews – the beach, the posh hotel, the film crew. No one from the film company was around to say goodbye as I left the hotel – Marianne and the gang were up at the set, packing everything up. Jemima was flying out later, after her farewell lunch with the principal actors, and I had a long train journey ahead.

I stood on the curb, waiting for the car to take me to Leuchars train station, for the start of my journey south. A pair of students walked past, red cloaks flapping behind them, folders in arms, on their way to a lecture. It was like Hogwarts here, and I loved it for that.

What was my plan now? Go back to work for Jemima until I got paid for this job? When Leoni told me what I was getting paid for one day's work, I nearly screamed! It was so much money – enough to help me rent somewhere for a month. OK, it wouldn't last very long, but Frank had said there might be work for me on his next project, which would be so perfect. But until then, I could work for Jemima, collect her dry cleaning, book her hair appointments, nurse her ego. If I stayed with the Edens, I might meet more useful people, too. Who knew? And seeing

George was always a bonus. Just thinking about him made me smile. And that gorgeous house. It made sense to stay for as long as I possibly could. If only Mum could see me now.

The car pulled up and I climbed in. I texted Leoni, as we whizzed over the Forth Road Bridge into Edinburgh.

> Hi! Filming went so well. Thank you so much!!

Well, I'd got the job myself, but I suppose she had been quick to sort out the paperwork. Eager to get her 10 percent no doubt. I typed some more.

> I'll update my Spotlight profile. It might get me some more work? Frank said he had another film coming up I would be good for.

Dots appeared.

> That's so great. I'll get on to his production company.

Leoni was an enthusiastic agent now that there was work coming in. I leaned back and looked across the river. It was all coming together. At last.

THIRTY-EIGHT

JEMIMA

My flight is delayed, and the irritating man next to me is listening to old-man rock, which seeps out of his headphones. It takes ages to get a drink, too – hopeless. In the row behind me, a couple are chatting and laughing, watching a TV show together on a phone. I feel sure they recognised me when they boarded. He definitely whispered to her as I sat down.

George and I had been like those two at the start. We didn't have any money then, but we were such a team. We had the same ambitions and dreams, a shared view of the world. With George, I'd felt so safe; he exuded confidence, knew everyone, could talk to anyone.

We met at a dinner party in an old posh house in Hampstead. I'd had a tiny part in an ITV drama, and I'd been invited to dinner at the director's house. I'd been a bit worried at first – none of the other cast had been invited. But I'd gone anyway, had dressed up. To my relief, there were loads of people there, including George.

Really, George is not my type at all. Not conventionally handsome, not like the men I'd slept with before, but he had something they didn't. Total confidence. He knew that he could fit in, anywhere he chose to be. People smiled when he spoke to them, laughed at his jokes, and he in turn made them feel good about themselves. His thick, dark hair and large brown eyes made him look almost wolfish, and he certainly noticed everything and everyone.

While we ate, two actors, sitting near the director, had realised they'd both been at Cambridge together. 'Oh, Footlights! Me too! Do you know Marcus? Oh my god, he has done *so* well.'

George and I glanced at each other, and in that moment, I was his. Without saying a word, we knew what the other was thinking: *We are not like these people.* As the evening got late, and people started to move to the garden to smoke, and I was thinking I should leave, he came straight over to me.

'Jemima. Shall we leave this crowd behind?'

'Bored of the party?' I replied.

'I just think you and I are going to be together for a very long time. So, we might as well start now.'

Does that sound like the most ridiculous line? He barely knew me. But it became very clear in those first few weeks that we were almost the same person. George had come from nothing, too, and his meteoric rise had left him feeling like anything was possible.

'We aren't like the others. Born into money. Everything handed to them. We've earned it, haven't we, Jemima?' And he was right. The people we mixed with, at parties, at awards ceremonies, at brunches, on holiday in the Balearics, they all told stories of how their families had supported them, paid for expensive schools, bought them a first house. We were different.

As I walk through into arrivals, I see the sign for Jemima Eden straight away, and one of George's regular drivers takes my cases, and leads me to where the car is parked right outside, much to a traffic warden's annoyance.

I'll be home before long, and George will be waiting.

THIRTY-NINE

KIM

George must have heard me banging my case up the stairs because the door opened, just as I reached it.

'You're back! Good to see you.' He took hold of my bag and lifted it into the hallway, then pulled me into an unexpected hug. 'I've missed my girls.'

'Jemima should be back soon. Her flight was late taking off, but it's about to land.'

'Great! Yes, I've been tracking it, too.'

He followed me into the kitchen and watched me get a glass of water.

'Thank you, Kim, for keeping an eye on her up in Scotland. I appreciate it.'

'No problem.' I'd hardly done anything, but he seemed happy. I noticed he had a bottle of wine open.

'How did your scene go?'

'Great! It's very small, but I loved doing it.'

'And how was Jemima about it?' He raised his eyebrows.

'She wasn't enthusiastic at first. But she was fine...'

George looked at me, as if we were both thinking the same

thing. Jemima had to be supportive really; she would have looked a real diva otherwise.

'Good for you! I'm sure Frank thought you were marvellous.'

Jemima wouldn't be back for a while, and I was acutely aware that it was just George and I in the house again. It felt nice to come home to someone who was so pleased to see me. I hadn't felt like that in a long time. I realised I was staring at him.

'I'll take my stuff downstairs. Let me know if you need anything,' I managed, before scuttling out of the room.

ACT 3

FORTY

JEMIMA

'Why are they coming today? I only got back from filming yesterday.'

'I did tell you about this. It's in the shared calendar.'

It wasn't, last time I looked. I'd remember if George's annoying, perfect sister was coming over.

'They should be here, for one.'

'Maybe you should cancel them. After last night...' How could he act like everything was OK, so normal? I could still feel where he had pushed me. He had apologised, as usual, but the atmosphere between us is still loaded and tense. And he wants his sister and kid to come here today?

'It's the best day for me, before I go away. I haven't seen her for ages.' He smiles, clearly delighted at the prospect of his two favourite people coming over.

I guess, in a way, the disagreement was my fault. He'd wanted sex when I got in, and I hadn't. And then I'd turned away to check my phone, and all hell had broken loose. I shut my eyes at the memory. George never used to be like that.

I get dressed into jeans and a soft, comfy sweater, and then carefully apply make-up to remove any traces of the night before. My creams and powders are so soft, they glide over my skin, turning everything flawless. There. I look so much better, more in control.

Kim is tapping away in my office, and smiles at me as I walk in. She's here early, but that's probably a good thing. Kim being in the house means that George has to be on his best behaviour.

'You've got a nice request for an interview with *The Times*. Do you want to do it?' she asks, peeking out from behind the screen.

'Sure. It's been a while.'

'Great. I'll set that up for you.'

'Kim, can you pop out and buy some toys suitable for a five-year-old? Nothing noisy or irritating. Something that will keep a kid busy for an hour or two.'

'Yes, of course. Now?' She looks confused.

'Yes. George's niece and sister are coming over. Terrible timing. I'm so tired from filming. He never thinks of things like that.'

'Of course. Do you need anything else while I'm out?'

She's looking at me very closely. Has she seen the bruising? 'No. I'm fine. Thanks for asking.'

At one on the dot, Heather and Joanna arrive. Heather is always on time, never late, that isn't her style. She's an accountant; always so predictable.

'Joanna! Come here! Not too big to be picked up, are you?' George doesn't wait for an answer, and swings Joanna into the air as soon as she steps inside the house. The spitting image of her mother, but in miniature, Joanna clearly adores Uncle George. I barely get a hello. I make a mental note to buy the little girl something decent to wear for her next birthday. No kid deserves to go out in public dressed like that. Mauve does not work with her hair colour.

Kim appears in the kitchen doorway and offers tea, which Heather seems thrilled by, introducing herself. Is it too early for wine? I don't think so. It can only help. I go over to the fridge and pour myself a large glass. I swear Heather gives me a look for it, which only makes me enjoy it more.

'She's so adorable! She's grown, right?' George watches as Joanna runs across the kitchen, and climbs onto our velvet sofa. She could have taken her shoes off.

'Well, it has been a couple of months since you saw her.'

'I'm so sorry! You know what it's like. I've been filming, working away. Jemima gets so fed up, I'm away so much.'

Sure I do.

'How's work for you, Heather?' I ask, hoping that she won't go into too much detail. But no, we got a long run-down of the latest issue in financial regulations, which I am sure is fascinating if you are into that sort of thing, which clearly we are not. George does manage to nod in the right places, so delighted to have his sister here. Joanna, in the corner of the room, is pulling leaves off a very expensive yucca plant.

'Kim, did you get some toys?' I ask. Kim is busying herself tipping salads into bowls.

'Yes, I did. Sorry. I'll go and get them.'

'So funny you having *staff*, George,' Heather says, as soon as Kim leaves the room.

'Kim is Jemima's PA. Been here a while now.'

'And she makes lunch, too? Is that related to your acting work?' Heather smiles at me, the smile not quite reaching her eyes. She's never approved of me.

'She's just helping, as you're here. We need a housekeeper, too, George, really.' I say that to wind Heather up. And it works. It's just her and Joanna at home, since Nick left her. I'm sure George helps her out financially. It's never really discussed, but there's no way she could afford private school fees on one salary. Only the best for darling Joanna.

'Here you go.' Kim kneels down next to Joanna, and proceeds to pull out toy after toy. A Barbie, some Lego, felt pens, colouring book, a plastic camper van. Goodness, how much has she spent? On my credit card. Joanna is clearly delighted and throws her arms around Kim. Easily bought, that one.

'Well, that buys us some time to enjoy lunch. Wine, Heather?' I hand her a glass, and offer to pour.

'Oh. No not for me. I'm on a health kick.'

I shrug and pour myself another.

'Steady on, darling. We could do with being a bit healthier ourselves!' Well, George can fuck off. He can drink anyone under the table. Since when did he care how much either of us drinks?

Heather looks delighted at this. 'Oh, are you two trying?'

Trying what? Do I look like I needed to be healthier? Then I realise, with a jolt, that she means something else entirely.

'Yes, we are.' George beams at her. 'It would be good to have a child to play with Joanna, wouldn't it?'

'You need to get a move on, then!'

I look at him, then at Heather. George knows what I'd been through. What we've both been through. Clearly he has kept this from his darling sister. I take another sip of wine to stop me saying anything I'll regret.

George leans over, and placed his hand on top of mine. A little too firmly. 'Steady, darling.'

'You'd need to cut back on the wine. Terrible for fertility,' Heather chimes in. 'And as you head towards forty, it gets harder to get pregnant. You can't leave it too late.'

How old does she think I am?

'I'd love another child. Of course I would...' And to my horror, Heather started to cry. George rushes to her side, and pulls her into a bear hug.

'That Nick is a bastard. You can do so much better.' I watch the two of them, the very picture of perfect siblings. Over on the floor, Kim is playing with Joanna, pretending to drive the camper van. Do I want that? A small kid around the place? I look at George. *No. Not now*. Was this whole charade of playing happy families for my benefit? Well, there is no way on earth that I will agree to that. Not now.

FORTY-ONE

KIM

George's sister and niece came over, the day after Jemima got back from filming. Oh my god, she is such a cute kid! It'd been ages since I played with a small kid like that. I did a bit of babysitting when I was a teenager, and loved it. I was told off for keeping them up too late, when they were meant to go to bed. Mum always told me that I would make an amazing mother. And, yes, I hope that one day I will have my own children. That seems like a million years away though, right now. I've just got my first acting job, and that needs to be my focus now.

But Joanna was adorable, playing with her toys, then eating the pasta I made for her. Jemima and George had no idea what to do. They had all their usual salads in the fridge, all quinoa, chickpeas, pomegranate and things like that, and I knew there was no way a five-year-old would like that, so I quickly knocked up a tomato sauce and found some pasta, and she was delighted with that.

'You're such a natural with children,' George had said. His sister was lovely, too, such a kind, friendly face. It was funny seeing them all eating together. Jemima was like the total opposite of Heather. Jemima was so thin, angular almost, with that long, straight red hair. Heather was round, bubbly, curly dark hair, so like her brother in that way, I guess. Funny how men choose their partners, isn't it? From looking at him, you would never have known that Jemima would be his type.

I was worn out from crawling around on the floor with Joanna, and glad to get back down to the basement, away from the noise for a while. Joanna had clung to me, in a bearhug, as they'd said their goodbyes in the hallway. I noticed that she didn't hug Jemima. They'd barely spoken to each other. Clearly not the maternal type.

I could hear George and Jemima bickering upstairs after they'd gone. You could tell Jemima hadn't enjoyed having Heather and Joanna over – really, she could have acted her way through it for the sake of harmony.

It was funny working here. I got to see that, however famous people might be, at home, they were really just like you and me. That however perfect something looks like on the outside, it isn't always like that in reality.

FORTY-TWO

JEMIMA

George has been completely foul since his sister left. I played the perfect wife, didn't I? Listened to Heather bore on about her job, about her marriage woes, about so desperately wanting another baby. She barely paid attention to the one she already had! Poor Kim picked up the slack there, playing for hours with Joanna. She has been useful today, I have to give her that. Clearly she can also add childcare to her list of many skills.

I lie here, with the bulk of George snoring away next to me. He hasn't demanded make-up sex, so that's one positive. It's just a few days until he goes away to Cannes, and then I can have the house to myself for a week. Blissful. Maybe I'll give Kim the time off, and it will be solely mine. She's probably due some time off anyway. We'd never really pinned that side of things down.

Maybe Rory could come over. It's been a while since we texted in Scotland, and surely he's got over that whole thing by now. A loud snort erupts from George. He didn't use to snore. Or maybe it's me not able to sleep so well as I used to. It's crazy to try and sleep here, when we have numerous spare rooms available.

I slide out from under the covers, as quietly as I can, then walk across the room. With a loud flop, George rolls onto his back, filling the space I've left behind. The snoring will be even worse now. I walk quietly along the corridor to the small room at the end, overlooking the garden. I slide between the cool sheets, and stretch out as much as I can in a single bed. This room would have been perfect. I always feel closer to her when I'm in here.

When I think back to where I grew up... that tiny council house on the outskirts of Bristol. And then Seagrass, that old canal boat I lived in during my early twenties. It would have been so different for my own children. She would have had everything.

It's amazing to think that just one acting job got me the deposit for this place. We've worked hard to pay for it ever since. It should be filled with family, with joy and happiness. I would have placed the changing table there, and the book-shelves over there, and I would have found a doll's house that would have fit perfectly under the windowsill.

George was so charming when we first met. Like *he* was the lucky one, to be going out with me. Always such a gentleman, making sure I was OK, that I had everything I wanted when we went out for dinner. Introducing me to people at the industry events we went to. We made such a great team, thrilled for each other when something went well, when one of us got a part.

I remember when he took me to the BAFTAs, as his date. I had panicked about what to wear, but George had said that I would look beautiful in anything. I spent hours searching for the perfect outfit, so I would look the part. I'd chosen a green silk dress, and paid more than I ever had for one thing before – I had mostly bought second-hand until then. It fitted me perfectly, and when I put it on and got ready to go out that night, I felt truly special.

I lie here, in bed alone, and think back to that night. George had been nominated for a best supporting actor role, though it was a small part in an indie film. He was so excited, like a puppy! He had picked me up in a long black car, with tinted windows, paid for by the production company, and we sat in the back together. As we pulled up to the Royal Albert Hall, I could not believe the noise and chaos that greeted us. Crowds lined the roads, waiting to see the stars arriving. Overhead lights made the sky glow orange, and as we pulled up in front of the building, I could see enormous cameras, waiting to film the arrivals.

'You OK?' he asked sweetly, checking on me, when I was the one meant to be supporting him! A man opened our car door, and we stepped out to flashing lights. I felt George's hand on my back, and he whispered to me, 'You look incredible.' We were swept inside the building, George waving and smiling to the crowd. In the foyer, he seemed to know everyone, and they were all happy to see him, smiling, hugging him, congratulating him on his nomination. And he proudly introduced me to the team who had made the film.

'This is Jemima Evans, an actor. And my girlfriend, would you believe!'

'Punching above your weight, there, George,' one man said to him, and George laughed and agreed. We had our photo taken together so many times, and then we were shown to our seats. I fully expected to sit somewhere near the back, as surely the seats at the front were for the really famous people, but no, we were shown to two seats, about three rows from the stage. I was right next to George.

'Hello, mate!' Guy Ritchie leaned across the seat, and hugged George. He'd been in the film, too. And then Kate Winslet arrived and sat next to me! She was up for best actress. She chatted away to George like they'd known each other for years. And then the lights went down, and you could sense the palpable excitement in the room. The awards were due to start.

George leaned close to me and said, 'We belong here. You know that, right?' And he held my hand, and it was the most magical feeling.

I should have known how things would turn out. He didn't win that night, and the mood in the car on the way back to his house was very different. I tried my best to cheer him up, but my words fell short of what was needed. Staring out of the window, as the lights of London flowed past, he almost looked like a sulky child, but I could hardly blame him for that, could I? I mean, how would I feel if I had lost? And a whole room of your peers was there to witness it.

The man who had won the award came up to George in the foyer afterwards, and said some lovely words, and I saw then what a good actor George is. He congratulated Simon Openshaw, told him that his work was outstanding, and his film was so important and that he thoroughly deserved the award. The two men had hugged and promised to meet up.

There had been talk of an after-show party, and I would have loved to go, but clearly George was eager to leave. Fair enough. My job was to support him. Play the dutiful girlfriend. And back then, I was so happy to play that role. I felt grateful to be there, to be with him. In the car, I had tried to say the right things, to tell him how amazing it was to be there, to be in the room with those people.

He'd turned and snapped at me. 'You seemed very smitten with Simon Openshaw. You couldn't stop smiling at him.' Gone were his sparkling, friendly eyes, and instead, he stared at me, all warmth gone.

'No. Not at all. He was talking to you. I was just trying to be nice.'

'I could see the way he looked at you. In that dress.'

I felt my hand go up to my chest, to cover myself. 'I'm here with you, George. You should have won.' That seemed to placate him, but I knew something had changed between us.

We'd had sex that night, and it was different... He barely spoke to me, and was rougher than ever before. And then he'd rolled off me, turned his back. I tried to hug him, to offer comfort after his night of disappointment, but he'd pushed my hand away.

He went back to his usual charming self the next morning, bringing me breakfast in bed, tea and toast with marmalade. My favourite. It was sweet that he had remembered that.

He used to bring toast to me when I felt queasy in the mornings, too. That all feels like a long time ago.

Out in the garden, a bird of some kind hoots. Feeling restless, I part the curtains and look out onto the garden below. Lit by moonlight, it's such a large garden for the city. I can see a fox, lying there, bathing in the moonlight. *Better not hang around too long, lovely fox.* George hates them, calls them vermin. But I just see a beautiful creature, trying to find a place to call home.

FORTY-THREE

KIM

'Morning, Kim! How are you this fine morning?' George was in gym kit, which suited him.

'Really well, thank you. I'm organising Jemima's expenses today, and then I've got a meeting later with Leoni.'

'From Elle's agency, right?'

I nodded. 'The director in Scotland has a part that he wants to see me for.'

'That's amazing! I'm so glad that all worked out for you.'

'They are having a wrap party at the weekend, the whole cast and crew from Scotland. The production company emailed me about it.'

'How glamorous! Somewhere fabulous, I hope?

'Frith Street House? Not been there before.' Obviously I hadn't been there before. It was a posh member's club in London.

'And Jemima will be going?' George asked.

'Yes, think so. I'm sure you would be welcome to come, too.'

I was really looking forward to it. It would be good to see Marianne again, and the rest of the crew. It would be useful to be in the same room as Frank, too, remind him that I existed, and I could maybe mention the other project. It felt like it was all coming together for me.

'Sounds great. Pop it in our joint calendar.' George grabbed a banana from the counter, peeled it and ate it in three large bites. 'I really appreciate you staying in touch in Scotland. I would have been so worried otherwise. It made me feel better knowing you were there, with her.'

'It was no problem.'

He threw his banana peel in the bin under the sink. 'And you were so great with Joanna, yesterday, thank you. She loved having someone to play with. Gave my sister a chance to relax.'

'That age can be so full-on. I enjoyed it.'

He laughed. 'It really can. She's a great kid though. You worked with kids before? You're clearly a natural with them.'

'I did a lot of babysitting when I was younger. Lots of kids on our estate.'

'How lovely. I can see you doing that.' He looked thoughtful for a moment. 'I can't wait for Jemima and I to have children. I had hoped it would be sooner, to have at least one that would be similar in age to Joanna. Too late for that, of course, but, well, we've still got time to start our own family.'

I had never heard Jemima talk about wanting kids. But then, she wouldn't to me, would she? And she had shown very little interest in Joanna yesterday. But sometimes people who desperately want a child find it difficult to be around other people's children. I remember when Mum couldn't have any more. Dad had left, and it was just us two. It suited me. But I noticed the sad look in her eyes when we were visiting family who'd just had a baby. We stopped seeing them often after that.

George placed his coffee cup in the dishwasher, always tidy. 'Well, you have a good day. Hope the agent chat goes well. You know, you remind me so much of Jemima. When she was just starting out. Exciting times.' He smiled at me, so encouraging.

'Let me know if I can help with anything. Got to show those agents who's boss!'

Just as he reached the door to the hallway, he turned to look at me. 'Could you ping over Jemima's expenses when you've finished please? Probably a lot of overlap with mine. I can send them to my accountant, too.'

Before I had a chance to reply, he grinned. 'You are such a treasure. Thank you.'

It was mid-morning when Jemima finally made it downstairs. That woman loved a lie-in.

'Morning! Can I get you anything?'

'Some peace and quiet please, Kim.'

Well, that told me. I started to pack up my laptop and paperwork to leave the kitchen. Shame, as I liked working in here on a sunny morning. Jemima poured a glass of water and drank with her back to me. I noticed she was leaning on the counter – heavy night? She had clearly drunk more than George who was, by contrast, positively perky.

'Jemima, I've got an appointment at four so I started early today. I hope that's OK. I'll need to leave about half three.'

Jemima turned to look at me. She did look rough. Pale skin, with grey shadows under her eyes.

'That's fine, Kim. Not too much to do here anyway.'

That was very unlike her.

'I'm sorting out your expenses. And we both got an invitation to the wrap party of our show! I've printed it out for you.'

'Our show.' She looked away. 'Thanks.'

'I mentioned it to George. It did say plus one. Well, I mean, it sort of came up when we were talking this morning.' As I spoke I had the strong sense that somehow I had been disloyal. I wasn't entirely sure who to.

'He does love a party.' Jemima smiled at me, and placed her

glass next to the sink. I noticed, with a start, that there was bruising on her arm. As if sensing me staring at her, Jemima pulled down her sleeve. For just a split second, she looked fragile, as if the slightest thing could knock her-off course.

'Are you OK, Jemima?' I regretted the words as soon as they left my mouth.

'I thought you were leaving, Kim.' Jemima glanced at my folded laptop.

'Yes, sorry, of course. I'll let you enjoy your breakfast.'

FORTY-FOUR

KIM

'Kim! So good to see you!' Leoni indicated for me to sit down. 'So, how was Scotland? Freezing cold, hanging out in castles all the time?'

She opened a drawer in her desk. 'How about whisky, as you've just been up North?' Without me replying, she poured us both a tumbler of whisky, like that was entirely normal behaviour in an office.

'Let's make a toast. To Kim Conner. On her first professional acting job!' Leoni took a sip and winced. 'Heavens, that stuff is strong. A gift from a client.'

I tried mine. Not too bad, quite warming. I was eager for her to get to why she wanted to see me.

'So, we've been sent a play script. I thought you might be interested.'

I sat up. 'I thought I was here about Frank's new project?'

Leoni shook her head. 'That will be next year, at the earliest. No, I want to talk to you about this. It's a play. A short run at Soho Place, London. Sounds good.'

I took the script she was holding out. 'Take your time. Give it a good read and get back to me later.'

A play! This was incredible.

'I'd love to. Thanks!'

Leoni laughed. 'I like your enthusiasm, but you'll need to audition first. And I do need to fill you in on something else, too...'

Leoni took a moment to gather her thoughts. 'This script has been sent to Jemima as well. For one of the lead roles, of course.'

I looked at her, puzzled.

'I'll just come out with it. Would you two be OK working together on this? It's an unusual one, but you are both our clients. The director saw you on our website, and asked to audition you.'

Jemima wouldn't like the idea, I was sure. She hadn't shown much genuine interest in my acting role up in Scotland. I thought of Jemima in her trailer in St Andrews, panicking over learning her lines. I couldn't imagine her being able to do a play, live every night, without making mistakes.

'Leoni. Have you and Elle spoken to Jemima about it? Does she want to do it?' Surely they had asked her first.

'Oh, yes of course. Elle will be all over that.' I had the strong feeling Leoni was keeping something from me. But I wasn't in a position to ask too many questions.

'I'm happy to try for it. If Jemima is OK with it. Thanks for the opportunity.'

'Great! It might all work out perfectly. Top up?'

FORTY-FIVE

JEMIMA

'I think you could do this play. Shall I put you forward?' Elle sounds very enthusiastic on the phone.

'I don't know, Elle. It's been a while...'

'You did specifically ask me to look at theatre. And in your last play you were so good! Maybe it's time you stepped back onto the stage. It's a nice play, not too demanding. It's worth throwing your hat in the ring.'

'How long is the run for?'

'Six weeks. They might extend. Depends how it goes.'

'Who else is in the cast?'

'No idea yet. They will need to cast two men, older. Why is that always the case? The women are always younger than the men. Male playwright...'

I can almost hear Elle roll her eyes.

'How many lines?' I ask.

It's been so long since I've learned a whole script and done a play. Filming is different, you can redo the lines if you mess one up. My mind goes back to Scotland, and the look on Frank's face as we had to do yet another take.

'Hmmm, about seventy lines? Not actually that many. No huge, long speeches either. You would have to play the piano for a few moments – how perfect is that! I know you have been having lessons. Honestly, Jemima, if you are considering ever doing a play again, this is the one.'

I rub my arm. The bruise is turning into a disgusting yellow. I feel sure Kim noticed it yesterday.

'OK. I'll consider it. Can you send me the script please? And you'd better send me the music, too.' It *would* be a chance to show my skills... could I do it?

'Great! It will be good to get you back on the stage. And, Jemima? Kim is in the running for the younger role.'

That throws me for a moment. I know Kim is with the same agency, but she's barely acted.

'Is she? Wow, that's... well, clever Kim.'

'No idea if she will get it, but it would be good to have someone there with you. To support you, if needed. It could work out perfectly.'

'I don't need support.' I'm more than capable of doing this play without my PA hovering around me. What's Elle implying? That I can't do this without help?

'Oh heavens, of course not! Only in the most lovely way. It's so great to know who you are working with... to keep it in the family, as it were. Nice for us as an agency. But she might not be right for it anyway.'

I look around my office. I need to keep the money coming in to pay for this house, that's for sure. And I'd wanted this, hadn't I? I can't stay perpetually cooped up here.

'OK. I'll try.'

I swear I can almost feel Elle smiling down the phone, before she hangs up.

So, Kim is up for this play, too. I walk over to the window. I have to admire that girl's tenacity. And Elle is right, she could be useful to me, helping me rehearse. But really, I need her here, looking after the house, especially if I'm going to be busy performing. She can't be in the same play as me. No, Kim is needed here. It's a shame for her, really, but there will be more opportunities.

Right now, I need to focus on me.

FORTY-SIX

KIM

It was chaos in the house. The wrap party for our Netflix series was on Friday night, and Jemima had me running around picking up outfits for her, none of which seemed to be right. It would have been so much easier if she could just go to a shop like anyone else and try things on. I needed to pick out an outfit as well – it was my party, too, though Jemima seemed to have forgotten that. On top of that, we both had to prepare for the auditions for the play in London. And didn't I know it – the sound of bad piano-playing echoed through the house. I noticed that the books on her piano were for grade three. That didn't seem very high to me.

I needed to learn my lines, and it wasn't easy with the noise, and Jemima also wanting to run her lines, but I was running out of time, so I took my script down to the basement. We had been sent different scenes to prepare, and Jemima expected me to help her as priority. Whenever I tried to learn my part, Jemima's voice kept swimming around in my head, confusing me. It was so frustrating – this part was perfect for me, and I knew how many other young actors would be trying for it. But I also had an in, because of Jemima. It crossed my mind that Jemima could help me prepare for my audition, but she never offered, so I didn't push my luck.

But I could learn from her, right? I had now spent hours watching Jemima say her lines. It was magical watching her. The way she held her face as she spoke. The way her voice changed, bringing emotion to every line. I could do that, right? I tried my lines again, as if it were Jemima doing them. *Hmm, yes, better.* I had never really understood when people said they had a 'good' side and a 'bad' side, but I did look better slightly side on. I turned off the light in the basement and left just a slant of natural light illuminate my face. In this soft light, I did look more interesting, the angles on my face sharper, more like her. I could imagine standing on the stage, lit by professionals, showing myself to the audience out there. I just needed to nail this audition, and that really could be me, standing there. And who knows who could be watching? A famous director perhaps? An influential critic? And George would come along, too.

I needed to get a grip. The part wasn't mine yet. If they wanted a star like Jemima Eden in this play, then what were the chances of them casting an unknown like me? Even though my part was much smaller, they'd want someone known, wouldn't they?

'Kim, are you down there?'

I'd been so absorbed in my lines that I hadn't heard the piano-playing stop.

'I want to run my lines again!' Jemima yelled down the stairs, sounding irritated. She must have been texting me.

My heart sank, but I got to my feet. I was only getting these opportunities because of her, and I needed to remember that. I put down my script, and went to help Jemima.

. . .

'Your car is confirmed for eight,' I told Jemima, who was sitting at her dressing table, having her make-up done.

'Great, thank you so much, Kim! You're an angel.' Her reflection in the dressing room mirror beamed at me. She was always so much nicer to me when someone else was there.

I closed the door, dismissed. Time to get myself ready. Jemima hadn't offered for me to go in the car with her, which was awkward. Was it just assumed I would go to the party with Jemima and George, or was I to make my own way there? I wasn't sure I could ask directly. Although I was in the film, Jemima never mentioned me attending. It was so odd. If I was going to get there on time – the invite said 8.30 p.m. – then I would need to leave about 7 p.m. if I was travelling by bus. In the car, I'd have more time.

I texted Marianne to ask what she was wearing, and was relieved when she replied quickly.

> Hey!! So glad you are coming! Jumpsuit
> probably? Wear anything you like!! See you
> later xx

Jumpsuit... OK, maybe a shirt of some kind would do, with loose trousers? But I did want to look my best, make a good impression, so that felt wrong, too. I went through Jemima's cast-offs again. I hadn't noticed this dress before. Older than some of the items, clearly worn a few times, from Whistles, so nice but not flash or anything. But really lovely. Dark green, strappy, but plain. Not real silk, but felt like it. This would be perfect, if it fit me. I could wear a denim jacket over it to tone it down if I needed to. Green was good with red hair, too right? A cliché, but nothing wrong with that.

I stripped down to my underwear and slipped it on, willing it to fit. OK, a little snug over the hips but it was good. Black ankle boots, or something dressier? I could feel anxiety starting to rise. I really wanted to fit in, look right. I had never been to a party like this before, and I wanted to look like I belonged there. Most of the team up in Scotland had only seen me in jeans and a padded coat, so it felt good to think they'd see me in a new light. Jemima had her hair piled up, and that looked good, had showed off her long neck. I could try that? Yes, better. Red lipstick. I had to say, looking in the mirror, I look alright. I smiled to myself.

Louella was in the hallway when I got upstairs, packing to leave.

She let out a low whistle. 'You look good! Where you off to?'

'Thanks! Same party as Jemima.'

'How fabulous! Nice perk of the job!' She grinned at me as she left, bags banging against the door frame. I really wanted to correct her, and say that I was an actor, too, a guest in my own right, but she had long gone.

'She's right. You do look amazing.'

I turned to see George standing at the bottom of the stairs. 'Wow, that dress on you... You look beautiful, Kim. The colour really suits you.'

'Thanks.' I felt a bit sheepish, standing there, him clearly staring at me. George looked pretty good himself. Charcoal jeans, blue shirt, and a tailored jacket. It was exactly the right balance of creative, yet expensive. He stepped towards me, and for a moment, I thought he was going to reach out and touch me.

'That's my dress.'

Jemima appeared at the top of the stairs. George and I turned to look at her. Slowly, she descended the stairs, her hand trailing along the banister, every bit the famous actress.

'I thought I recognised it.' George said, looking at me.

'Is it OK if I wear it? It was in one of the bags you said to give away.'

'And yet, clearly you didn't do that.' Jemima was now standing just a few steps away from me.

'You look lovely, darling,' George said, and kissed Jemima on the cheek. She barely registered it.

Did she want me to go and change? I stood there, feeling stupid. It was just an old dress – she had so many new dresses to choose from, better dresses, more expensive. Surely she didn't really care about this one?

'Shall we have a drink before we go?' George said, and I loved him for that, trying to diffuse the tension. He took Jemima's arm, to lead her to the kitchen, and I noticed she flinched, just for a second.

'I need to get going...' I said, eager to get on my way.

'Oh? Are you not coming with us?' George asked, looking momentarily puzzled.

'I'm getting the bus.' Damn, I should have asked Louella if she was heading towards the city centre, got a lift with her.

'Bus! That's ridiculous. Come with us. Don't you think, Jemima?'

Jemima looked at me, her carefully made-up face was so beautiful, immaculate, but there was a coldness in her eyes that made me uncomfortable. And then she broke into a smile, transforming her face entirely.

'Of course! Now, you said something about a drink, George? We need something to help us get us in the mood.'

FORTY-SEVEN

JEMIMA

At least George and Kim know to walk behind me as we make our entrance into Frith Street House. I'm still the big name here. Most people wouldn't know that the Frith Street Members' Club existed – a black Victorian door, like so many others on this road, with a discreet brass doorbell, without any signage to say what's hidden away inside. Most people just walk on past and have no idea of the stars who make this their base when in London. Film directors, TV executives, advertising moguls, and, of course, the actors who everyone is really interested in, all come here for private meetings, late night drinks, and more. I've experienced many memorable nights here. The Grade-II listed townhouse feels like coming home. Although, of course, our house is bigger.

'Good evening, Mrs Eden, Mr Eden.' The doorman nods at us. Sweet that he welcomed me first, even though George is by far the more regular visitor here now. When *was* the last time I was here? It feels so good to be out and about. We're shown along the familiar corridor, past a Tracey Emin and a Yinka Shonibare. I do love Tracey Emin and her whole story. In some ways, we have things in common – her humble start in life and tough teen years, then her upward trajectory to becoming a household name. I know all about that life. I have two of her drawings in our bedroom. George hates them, of course.

The party is in full flow on the roof terrace. String lights bob in the breeze, highlighting the exposed brick walls all around us. A waiter hands me a glass of Champagne, and I noticed that he glances at my breasts before looking at George, sheepishly. I've made a good choice on the dress, then. Dark gold, draped fabric, I'd worried it looked a bit Grecian back at home, but here it looks just right. I am a leading lady, after all.

'Jemima!' Frank appears in front of me, and tries to hug me, which is a little awkward, as we are both holding glasses.

'And George!' Frank slaps George on the shoulder, in a manly gesture that doesn't suit either of them.

'Frank! I can't wait to see the film. The girls tell me it was great fun to work on.'

The *girls*. I swallow. This is not the time to react.

'Ah yes, great fun. Kim! How lovely to see you again. Our new star.' Frank leans over Kim and kisses her on both cheeks. I notice that he didn't tried to kiss me.

Kim looks quite something in that green dress. George's earlier reaction said it all. I notice she's wearing Converses with it, which I have to say, sort of works. I tower over her in my Manolos. I suddenly feel like I've tried too hard, got the vibe wrong.

'Kim!' Marianne, with her bra straps showing. She hugs Kim. George and Frank are chatting away loudly, and I watch as Kim and her friend join a group in the corner, clearly technical crew, a scruffy bunch. They all look delighted to see her.

Frank turns his attention back to me. 'Jemima. This is Joseph Sved. The man behind Park Productions.' A small man with a big smile leans towards me, expectantly. Why do these men always think women want to kiss them?

'Joseph is the finance behind our film. The money man.'

Frank beams at me. Oh, so I'm supposed to supply the charm, make this little man feel part of the glamorous crowd. I look across at Kim and her friends, all laughing over some shared joke. That looks like a more fun place to be right now.

'Joseph! Great to see you!' George, to his credit, strikes up conversation with the money man. This is much more his scene. I need another drink. That glass of Champagne has gone fast.

'Back in a moment.' I make my excuses and walk over to where a bar has been set up in the corner of the space, a DJ with a laptop balanced nearby. A beautiful woman with enormous brown eyes is behind the bar. Surely she's an actor, with that face? Or a model. Is she working here, hoping to get spotted? We all had to make ends meet, while we waited for our big break. I had done my time, for sure.

Martini in hand, I survey the scene. The party has clearly divided into groups, with the crew in one corner, Kim at the very heart of it. The middle-aged men have gathered around Frank, as if awaiting further instructions. Not many of the actors seem to be here. Too busy on other projects or just too cool to turn up on time?

The minutes drag, but I make small talk with people as they collect drinks from the bar. How long do I need to show my face, to fulfil my obligations? I order another martini.

'Jemima! How fabulous to see you. We weren't sure if you would pitch up.' Donald appears next to me, with Katherine right behind him.

'Of course! It's wonderful to see you both. Just got here?'

'We went for dinner. Didn't think this was your sort of thing,' Katherine smiles at me. She looks amazing, I have to give her that. A jumpsuit, short straps, in a silky fabric that fits her perfectly, but doesn't look too showy. I note that I wasn't invited to join them for dinner.

'Got to play the game,' I reply.

'Your PA seems to be quite the hit, doesn't she?' Donald nods in the direction of Kim. He has his hand on Katherine's waist. *Interesting.* Clearly they had got close on the film set. I wonder what Katherine's husband would make of that.

'I know! So great.' Kim is getting a lot of attention considering how small her part was. Though Donald probably means it as a compliment to me.

'So, what's next for you?' Katherine asks. The classic question that all actors hate. It's not like we can be busy all the time, it's hardly a nine-to-five job.

There is no way I'm telling her about the play. I've sent in a recording of me playing the piano, just to show Elle and the casting director that I can do that. Now I just have to wait and see if they make me an offer. Surely they will? I mean, I'm a big name. Enough to get backing for any project, to sell tickets, get bums on seats. I'm a shoo-in. It crosses my mind that Katherine could have been put forward for the same play. We are fairly close in age, and similar casting type, so it's a possibility.

'Oh, nothing right now. How about you?' I take a slug of my martini. God, I hope she isn't going to list all the amazing things she's working on. *Best smile, Jemima.*

'Oh, my goodness. I'm so busy!' Katherine smiles at me, delighted to be asked. 'I need to fly out to Miami tomorrow morning to do some PR for a film I did ages ago. I shouldn't be here really, I've got such an early start. And then straight to Germany for a meeting with a director. Very arty, that one. Oscar potential. I mean not for *me*, personally, of course! But it's got that credibility you know? For best film. I mean, here I am getting so ahead of myself! It is an amazing script though. Nice to get sent something decent, isn't it? Especially at our age.'

I really don't know what to say to that stream of boastfulness, but thankfully, Donald steps in to fill the silence.

'Oh, that sounds amazing. And you two are in your prime!'
Donald beams at us both. I try not to roll my eyes.

He leans in, whispering. 'You'll both think me so shallow,
but I'm filming a coffee commercial next. It's insane money, I
couldn't turn it down.' Donald grins. 'I can donate the money to
my new charity foundation.'

Oh god. So rich now that he can afford to give money away.
Of course he had to mention it, else what would be the point?

'Oh wow, that's amazing. Tell us all!' Katherine takes the
bait.

'Well, as I said, it's a new project. A charity to support up-
and-coming actors. Pay for their audition fees, that sort of thing.
It feels so good to give back, doesn't it? Well, you know what I
mean, Jemima. Here you are, supporting your protégé.'

'Yes, it really does.' I glance over at Kim. Just behind her,
George is hanging around, looking a little out of place talking to
the crew. Making himself look like a man of the people, I guess.
Mr Popular. One of the sound crew hands him a bottle of beer.
He hates Italian beer. I watch him laugh, and take a large swig.
He's the oldest by at least ten years.

'Another drink, ladies?' Donald indicates to the bartender,
who immediately leaves the two make-up artists who have been
waiting to order and comes over to us. Smart girl.

'Three martinis? Right?'

How long do I have to stay for? Katherine and Donald have
left me at the bar to chat to someone Donald knows. I could go
over to Frank, work some charm on him, find out if he had any
work going for me in the future. Yes, that's a good idea, and
then leave. No one else here is really worth talking to. I
wonder if they'll do speeches, thanking the stars and all that,
but Frank seems to be enjoying himself far too much to switch
into formal mode now. George is still busy working the room.

Will he come home, if I tell him I'm leaving? He looks in no rush to go.

What's Rory doing right now, I wonder? His play isn't that far away, and it's the weekend, so he might well be out after work. I could leave, meet him somewhere for a nightcap. *Crazy thinking, Jemima. You're here to work and network, and George is right over there.* No harm in texting hello though, right?

> Hi stranger. Remember me? How's things? I'm in the club. Soho.

Perfect. Just friendly. The right tone. Rory will be amazed that I'm out – it has been so long since we hit the bars and clubs round here.

The DJ has got louder, and some of the crew are dancing now, having made the most of the free drinks. George is holding court on the far side of the room, oblivious to me still parked on a stool by the bar.

Dots appear on my phone. Rory!

> Excellent! Glad you are out xx Have fun xx.

Is that it? I type a quick reply.

> You still up? Nightcap?

Dots appear. And then stop.

Oh for fuck's sake. I slam my phone down on the zinc bar. A woman, a few steps away, turns to look at me. *Mind your own business. Well, screw you, Rory.* I call for another drink, which appears quickly. I pick out the olive and resisted the urge to throw it at the judgemental woman. Who is she anyway? No one I recognise. Nobody important. Delicious, cold vodka. Soothing and relaxing.

I should go and talk to Frank, do something useful. I stand

up, and feel the room lurch to one side, and I hear a gasp behind me. Just in time, I reach for the bar, and grip the cold, wet counter. I hear the bartender ask me something, but I couldn't tell you what it was. *Best I sit down again.* I smooth the hair from my face.

Water. I need a glass of water, and something to eat. A bowl of olives sits on the bar, shiny in their oil, little flecks of red pepper. I try to spear one with a tiny plastic sword.

'She's so drunk,' I hear.

'And no one to talk to. Sad really, isn't it?'

Were they talking about me? I turn, to try and see who said that. The woman standing near the bar? Or the group just along from me? But no, they're laughing and talking about something else.

'Took hours editing her scenes. So many takes.' It's a man's voice behind me. One of the crew I don't recognise. I stand up, wanting to tell him he's being a dick. How dare he talk about me, as if I wasn't there? Doesn't he know who I am?

'Jemima. You OK?' George, standing very close to me, his face serious. Is he angry with me? Well, screw him. I push past him, to make my way to the door. I can get a cab, get home myself.

'Hey, you ready to head home? Me too.' Kim appears next to me, and takes my arm, very gently, and then we're outside, and the air is so cool and refreshing.

A group of men walk past us, on the narrow pavement, Soho still very much alive at this time of night. 'Hey, isn't that—'

The flash of a phone camera.

'Fuck off!' Kim shouts. Seconds later, we're in an Uber, making our way through a garden square, the two of us in the back of the car together.

'What about George?' I said.

'Oh, he was saying goodbye to Frank. Said for us to go home.'

'I need some water,' I mutter. Did the driver have to take the corners so fast? I feel like I'm going to be sick, right there, in the car.

'Here.' Kim delves in her bag, and pulls out a scuffed metal water bottle.

'Thanks.'

'We'll be home soon.'

FORTY-EIGHT

KIM

I've never seen Jemima like that before. It was a nightmare trying to get her up the steps into the house, her balancing against me, while I fumbled for the keys. I had a few seconds to sort out the alarm, which wasn't easy, with Jemima trying to help.

'Can I make you some toast?' I asked, helping her into the kitchen. Something to soak up some of the alcohol.

'I'm fine,' Jemima mumbled, though clearly she wasn't. Marianne and her friends had planned to go to a club after the wrap party, somewhere Johannes knew. I felt completely dressed right, and Marianne had her trainers on, too. There was so much talk about what they were all up to. Marianne was working on her own film, part of her diploma course, and I'd offered to be in it, if she needed anyone, and she seemed genuinely pleased. It was starting to feel like I'd actually made real friends. And yet here I was, helping Jemima, yet again.

'I'm going to bed,' Jemima slurred, as she kicked off her shoes. Well, that was a good idea anyway. How had she got so drunk? It wasn't like her – she was usually so controlled.

'Let me help you.'

We made our way up to her room, and she crawled under the duvet, still in that amazing dress.

'I'll get you some water.' She nodded at that.

I was looking for some painkillers when George walked in. 'Hi. You got home OK then?' he said.

'Hi. Yes, thanks. Jemima has gone to bed. I'm going to take these up for her. Might save her from a nasty hangover.'

'Nice of you. You really are very caring.' He walked over to a cupboard and pulled out a bottle of wine. 'Thanks for taking her home. I felt the need to say goodbye to Frank, try and smooth things over. Jemima isn't usually that embarrassing.'

Well, she hasn't really done anything that bad...

'The doorman called us an Uber. Sorry. Should we have waited for you? I wasn't sure what to do.' I watched him pour a large glass of red wine. Had I overstepped? I had just done what seemed right for Jemima.

George took a gulp of wine, and then reached for another glass, presumably for me? 'Oh, don't worry. We are all very used to Jemima's dramas. I'm sorry you had to see that. You did exactly the right thing. Join me? It's been a hell of a day.' He looked tired, as he removed his tie, and loosened his top button.

'I'd better take these up to Jemima.'

George put his glass down, and then placed his hand on mine. I felt a shiver pass through my body. What was he doing?

'Stay. Talk to me.'

I stood still, deciding what to do. I knew that, upstairs, Jemima was waiting for me. Or maybe she would she be asleep already. The clock on the oven ticked over to 1.30 a.m. How had it got so late? I took a step back, and he released my hand.

'Just one glass of wine. Nightcap?' George looked at me, with a lopsided smile.

'I'm not sure...' It felt like a really bad idea, hanging out here with George. He'd clearly been drinking a lot.

'I couldn't take my eyes off you tonight. You shone, like the star you are.'

I stood very still. He shouldn't be saying things like that to me. I glanced at the kitchen door, as if expecting to see Jemima standing there.

'You looked so happy, talking to your friends. And Frank said you were excellent up in Scotland. A very promising young actor.'

'He said that?' I paused.

'He did. You know, there are so many young actresses out there, trying to make it. But you've got something special. You remind us both of a young Jemima, we both agreed that.'

'That's really nice. I can only dream of being as successful as she is.' I sat on the stool nearest to him.

George moved a little closer. 'It wouldn't surprise me at all if you made it big. I can spot talent.'

He hadn't actually seen me act though. The film wasn't even out yet. *Come on, Kim, you aren't an idiot. Time to get out of here, get to bed yourself.* But George had other ideas. He reached out, and took my hand once more.

'I can help you. It's all about who you know in this business. You've done so much for us, for me, and I am only too happy to return that favour.'

I tried to pull my hand away, but his grip was firm.

'You look beautiful in that dress.' George laughed, softly. 'You know, Jemima wore that dress to the BAFTAs, the first time we went together.' He smiled at the memory. 'We've been so many times since then, of course, but I remember that night. And that dress. It gave me quite a shock to see you in it.'

I looked down at the dress. Why hadn't Jemima said something? I should have thrown it out, like she told me, donated it to a charity shop. Why hadn't she kept it, if it had special memories?

'Well, this is very cosy.' We both turned. Standing in the

doorway, wrapped in a floor-length Chinese robe, looking completely in control of the situation, was Jemima.

I yanked my hand back.

'Darling. How are you feeling? Kim has found you some aspirin.'

'How kind.'

I stood up, picked up the packet, my hand shaking. I walked over to her, held out the pills, like an idiot.

'Thanks.' She slipped them into her pocket. 'Kim. I'm sure you're desperate to get home. It's been a long night.'

'Of course.'

Jemima stood aside to let me pass her. The door closed behind me, and I paused in the hallway. Jemima clearly expected me to leave, but where would I go? I hadn't yet found anywhere else to live. They were too focused on each other to worry about me, so I tiptoed downstairs to the basement. George hadn't told her I was staying here, then. Would he tell her tonight? From the sound of the raised voices in the kitchen, it sounded like they had other things on their minds.

FORTY-NINE

KIM

'Kim? Hi! Morning. It's Leoni.'

My phone had woken me from a deep, hungover sleep. It had taken ages for me to drop off. The sound of Jemima and George arguing had kept me awake. I half expected an angry Jemima to come bursting into the basement at any point and turf me out, but George must have kept my secret. At some point it had gone quiet upstairs, and I must have crashed out.

'Hi, Leoni.'

'So, it's good news. About the play. They want to see you in person. I've been texting you all morning, why didn't you reply? Are you free later?'

I sat up fast, then regretted it, as my head swam. How much had I drunk last night? Not *that* much, surely. 'Sorry... Yes, that's amazing. Thank you so much.' I held my head, tried to focus.

'They are seeing people this evening, at the Soho Place theatre. Hope it's OK, but I said yes for you. You don't have anything else booked in, right?'

'I can do that. Thanks, Leoni. I had sent my self-tape off in a rush. They must have liked it!' What time was it? Almost eleven. How had I slept that long? I had never been late to work before. I stood up, looked around for clean clothes to wear. 'What time do I need to get there?'

'Five. Let me know how it goes!' She hung up.

I stood there, staring at my phone. An email from Leoni arrived seconds later, with details of the play, the theatre address, and the full script. Oh my god, this was really happening for me! I needed to get ready, read this through, get a shower. I should have asked Leoni if she knew how many people were still in the running, find out my chances of getting this part. I needed to get my shit together, find some strong coffee, wake up. It was all very rushed, which probably meant I wasn't first choice, but that was OK. I could almost hear Mum telling me, 'They want to see you, so you are in the running. Get up, sweetheart!'

No one was around when I went upstairs, which was perfect. I'd got away with my late start, and maybe Jemima would have a long lie-in and I could concentrate on reading this script. I wondered if Jemima would be called in tonight, too? She probably didn't have to do auditions like the rest of us. Someone like her just got the part, if she was free. One day I might be in her position, too.

I settled down to work in Jemima's office. The nutritionist delivered fresh meals, which I stacked in the fridge. No sign of Jemima, which was odd. Clearly the hangover was bad. I heard the front door bang early afternoon, and looked out to see George heading down the path. He clearly hadn't wanted to come and say hello to me. I thought of his hand on mine last night... What would have happened if Jemima hadn't walked in? I just knew at some point she would mention it to me. But I hadn't done anything wrong. I'd helped her home, been a good

PA to her. George hadn't come back by the time I was due to leave to get to the theatre, which felt like a relief.

As I closed the door, it crossed my mind that I should have told Jemima I was going to the casting. But then, if I didn't get the part, was it really worth the hassle? Or what if she had been turned down for it? How awkward would that be? I had to admit, that did feel slightly delicious.

Maybe I would get this acting job, and then I could stop working here. I'd have to anyway, if I was working full-time as an actor, going to rehearsals and all that stuff. I wondered how many more times I would be walking down these steps.

Soho Place looked nothing like a theatre. A modern glass and steel box, it looked more like the offices of an IT company, but the red neon sign told me, that yes, this was the right place. A woman at the box office desk glanced up from her laptop as I approached.

'Kim Conner. For the audition. For *Mosquitoes*?'

'I've got you down for five? You're keen.'

I wasn't that early, only about fifteen minutes. 'Take a seat over there.' She waved me over to an uncomfortable-looking armchair. *What a warm welcome*. Maybe she wanted to be in my position, rather than hers. Everyone who works in a theatre really wants to be on the stage, don't they? I needed this time to do some breathing exercises, centre myself, read over my lines again.

I picked up the script. *Mosquitoes* was about two sisters, one a scientist, and the other just seemed to be a mess. I had googled the play and regretted it immediately, when I saw that Olivia Colman had done this play before. *Great. No pressure, then.*

I glanced around the foyer, to see if anyone about my age was also hanging around, waiting for an audition. Giant light-bulbs hung from the ceiling, and posters advertising 'A triumphant new musical' hung on the wall next to me. There was a bar in the corner, and a sign indicating the way to 'Stars Restaurant'. It would be so cool to rehearse here, come up for lunch and eat there, maybe hang out with the other actors. And it could be me with my name on a poster!

I imagined how great it would be if I did get this play, and I could tell Marianne and everyone about it. I would truly be part of that crowd, one of them, the actors and creatives. No longer the PA. I tried to read the script again, but I was too nervous to settle. I could be called any minute. I took a deep breath in and then a slow exhale out, just like I had seen Jemima do before her self-tapes.

'Kim.' I looked up, startled. Jemima was walking towards me, her heels tapping loudly on the concrete floor.

I leapt up out of my chair. 'Hi! You here for the casting, too?'

'Evidently,' she replied, coolly.

'That's great! I thought you probably didn't need to do these. Someone like you would just get given the part.' *Oh, why had I said that.*

'It's good to come in and meet everyone. Show my face,' she replied.

'Oh yes, that makes sense.' I nodded. Jemima looked exhausted, like she'd barely slept. We both stood there for a moment, and I wondered if I should be the first to bring up last night. But something in Jemima's expression told me not to mention it. Just behind her, I saw a woman walk in and talk to the receptionist. I recognised her from TV.

'What time are you due in?' I asked.

'Elle said five.' Jemima looked at the woman and raised her hand, in a very discreet wave.

'I'm due in at five, too!'

'Oh great. Well, I will see you in there.' Jemima gave me a half smile and walked over to talk to the woman, who had the most astonishing cheekbones. She was a similar age to Jemima, so I guess she was competing for the older sister part. Two more women walked into the foyer, laughing, clearly friendly, and spoke to the receptionist. I sat there on my own, watching them all. They all seemed so relaxed, so used to this. *Thank god Jemima hadn't wanted to talk about last night – that would have been too much right now.* I could feel my heart start to thud. *Calm down, Kim, take a breath. Don't blow it by being scared.*

A few minutes later, a man with a shaved head walked into the centre of the space, and said with a loud, confident voice, 'Can I have Jemima, Sarah, Indira, Kim and Emerald, please?' He looked around the room, and I watched Jemima walk over to him. Indira Chapman – that was it. She'd been in loads of stuff, gritty TV dramas, that sort of thing.

'Jemima Eden! This is so cool. Lovely to meet you,' the shaven-headed man gushed. The other women followed, and I got up last. None of us looked like each other. Two were older than me, more Jemima's age, and one was my age but looked completely different, with darker skin, black hair. Yet they were casting for sisters? I wondered how they would decide between us all. How many other actors were they seeing today? I had no idea what my chances were.

'This way, ladies!' the man said, and we followed him along a corridor, each of us trying to act relaxed. Jemima led the group, a good two metres ahead of me, chatting confidently to the man, though I couldn't hear clearly what they said.

We were shown into a huge modern auditorium, with seating for at least 600 people. Blue chairs surrounded the stage, and we stood in the centre, lights shining brightly onto our faces.

'Hello, everyone!' a voice from the seats called out, and two men walked forward, both dressed entirely in black. 'So glad you could be here. I'm Bill, this is Vikram.'

'Jemima! So lovely to see you.' The one called Vikram

stepped onto the stage and ran over to hug Jemima, which she loved, making a big fuss of him in return. I noticed her glance at Indira.

'OK, we are going to put you into pairs, and run Scene One. Let's start with Sarah and Indira. The rest of you can take a seat and watch.'

'Goodness, this is like being back at drama school,' Jemima said to me, taking me by surprise. I guess she had to be nice to me, in front of everyone else.

'As you know, we need two women, to play our sisters. So it's all about the chemistry between you, so that the audience can believe you're related. Right, you two ready? Let's get going. Remember, this is a collaboration. We want you to enjoy this process. No pressure here. Just play, and see how it goes!' Bill sat down and beamed at Indira and Sarah. No idea what Sarah's second name was. She looked my age though, so I knew she was up for the same part as me.

Jemima and I took seats just along from Bill in the front row. 'Sarah is very good. We worked together years ago. She can be a total bitch though.' I turned to look at her. She stared straight ahead, clearly not expecting me to reply. Close up, I could see the dark shadows under her eyes.

We watched the scene playing out in front of us. Wow, they were good. They both knew the lines off book, and were already acting like they were sisters, so comfortable together. Vikram gave Sarah some direction, and she tried it again, just like he told her. They both looked so effortless up there, so professional – I was out of my depth. I wasn't sure I knew the lines that well. How long had they had the script? Longer than me, clearly.

'OK, next up. Let's try Jemima and Kim. Up you go.' I followed Jemima onto the stage, my heart pounding. *Try and calm down, Kim*, I heard my mum say. But this was very different to a dance show in our village hall, or a school play.

Jemima took her position in the centre of the stage, and I

saw her roll her shoulders back, and relax into position. She looked so at home here, on the stage. So in command of the space. I shuffled into place a few steps away from her.

'You two look so alike! That's great. OK, start whenever you like.'

Jemima's character went first. The sisters were talking about an ultrasound. One of them is pregnant. Me.

'It's completely safe,' Jemima said, looking at me, exasperated.

'Um, no, not actually, not completely,' I replied.

'In what way?'

'No, because you are going to shout at me.' I turned away from Jemima, to avoid her looking at me.

'I won't shout at you. When have I ever...' she said, walking towards me.

'They've done animal studies,' I replied.

A pause from Jemima. 'Oh hell, I can't remember the next part.'

I turned to see her walk off the stage to fetch her script, which she had left on a chair. I felt irritation rise up in me. It had been going fine, and now she had broken the flow. Surely the directors wouldn't like that. I watched them, making notes, heads together.

Jemima rejoined me on the stage. I could see the other women watching. If Jemima couldn't remember this scene, she was going to struggle to get through a whole play, being the lead actor, surely? I could see Indira watching Jemima, a relaxed smile on her face.

'Rats,' I said my line, picking up where we left off.

'Rats. Okay. And what did they find in these—'

We got through the scene, and then Bill asked me to sit down, and Sarah got up to read my lines alongside Jemima. She was instantly good and I could see that the new combination brought out something different in Jemima, too. It was a brutal process, all being in the room together, but I could see why they did it, to see who looked and sounded right together. We watched Jemima and Sarah run the scene twice.

'OK, lovely! Jemima, can you try it again? This time sitting over there,' Vikram called out.

I could not have been the only one to hear Jemima mutter under her breath, 'Is this really necessary?' as she walked over to a row of painted wood blocks.

She sat down, and smiled over at Vikram. Sarah fed her the line, and Jemima returned her line.

'A bit louder, please, Jemima!' Bill called over.

Jemima let out a loud sigh. 'Really? I could just move the blocks nearer.'

'Just try and project,' Bill replied.

I could see that Jemima's face had started to tense.

'Go from the start, thank you,' Vikram directed.

'Is this necessary? I mean, you've seen me do this scene a few times now.' Quiet descended in the theatre. I glanced over at the two men. Would they be OK with being spoken to like that?

'All part of the process, Jemima, darling. It's helpful for us to see it a few times.'

Jemima shrugged. 'OK. Once more, but I need to be out of here by six. I do hope that is OK,' she said, as if anything later was completely unreasonable. *Wow*. As far as I knew she didn't have anything important booked in her diary.

'Of course! Well, let's make the most of the time we have together, then,' Bill replied, sounding quite happy with the situation.

I left the theatre just after six – the casting pretty much ended as soon as Jemima left. Indira and Sarah left together, chatting away, ignoring me as passed. I looked across the square outside, to the river beyond. What now? Probably better to stay out of Jemima's way if she had gone straight home. I could see groups of friends sitting out on the grass, having picnics of gins in tins, crisps and sandwiches. Tourists taking selfies. A mum walking past with a toddler in a buggy. It was just me, among this sea of friends and families – who could I tell about my day, about my audition? I texted Leoni.

> Went OK!! Really nice directors. Jemima was there!!

Her reply came back quickly.

> Yes! Elle told me she would be. So glad it went well! I'll let you know when I hear xxxx

Well, that was that. I needed a drink. To go somewhere dark and quiet where I could sit and no one would notice I was on my own. Somewhere I could celebrate that I had just had an audition, with top directors and famous actors. That meant something, right?

I walked away from the river and the tourists, and found myself in an alleyway, with old stone archways either side, and train tracks running overhead. Just ahead was a doorway, with potted trees outside. I glanced inside – a cosy bar with seats running one side of the converted tunnel. A bar on the left, bottles lit by fairy lights. I chose a red velvet bar stool, and pulled myself closer. The bartender handed me a drinks list, showing his tattooed arms, a jungle of flowers and thorns.

I opened the menu, and with horror, noticed the prices. The barman stood by, watching, waiting for me to decide. I felt sure he could read my mind and knew I couldn't really afford to be here. Jemima wouldn't even have noticed these prices; she would have ordered anything she liked. I indicated the cheapest glass of wine on the menu.

I wondered where Jemima was now. Somewhere meeting

friends? I wasn't sure who she would call a close friend – she didn't seem to have many. But then, who was I to comment? I didn't have many people in my life either. We had that much in common, at least. The alcohol started to work its magic, and I felt my mood lift. I had done so well to get that audition. Amazing how life turned around – old me, working in that club, would never have imagined this! Having someone with me here to celebrate would make it even better, but who to call? George? No... Maybe Marianne. Couldn't harm to ask what she was up to.

> You free? I'm having drinks near London
> Bridge!!! Celebrating

Now, to make this drink last as long as possible. Right now, I couldn't afford more than one of these, but who knew? If I got the part, I could do this all the time.

FIFTY

JEMIMA

Rory is late. And to think I have rushed out of the audition to get here on time. He doesn't have long before curtain up tonight, so here I am, waiting for him in Joe Allen. Not a very discreet choice by Rory, but it is right by the stage door to his theatre, so I guess it is convenient, for him at least. I sit with my back to the entrance, facing the bar, so anyone walking in will only see the back of my head.

'Sorry, sorry!' Rory arrives at last, kisses me on both cheeks, and throws himself down into the chair opposite. He signals for a drink, confident the bartender knows his order.

'Interesting choice of meeting place,' I say. He looks fantastic, so relaxed and handsome in that easy-going way he always has.

'Oh, they're great here, used to actors. And I can be back in the theatre in moments.'

He thanks the waiter for his whisky and takes a sip.

'Should you be drinking that before a show?'

'Helps with the vocal cords! So, what's so urgent? You sounded pretty stressed in your message.'

'You hadn't got back to me. I was beginning to think you were ghosting me.'

He laughs, and I notice him glance around the room. It is busy with the pre-theatre crowd, mostly middle-aged women with shopping bags from the Covent Garden shops heaped around their feet.

Rory pulls his chair closer to mine, and wraps his arm across the back of my seat. 'You know what it's like when I'm working. Crazy hours.'

He has never been this slow to respond to messages before. Even when he is working. Once you get going in a show, there is usually plenty of downtime. And Rory gets bored very easily – he is usually the first to text me. He has definitely been avoiding me. Maybe all his time is taken up with that Cassie.

'I needed to talk to you. You weren't returning my calls.' I sound desperate, which is not a good look. I take a sip of my martini to add a dramatic pause. 'I've been busy, too. Just had an audition. For a new play.'

'Oh wow, fantastic! Tell me all!' I forgive him slightly, as the martini kicks in. This is nice. Sitting here with Rory, talking about the play, the audition, the role.

'Indira was there. She was good, so she might get it.'

'Oh, don't worry at all. You are so much better! Totally different league.'

That is why it is so important to see Rory. He gets acting. He knows the acting world. It is so good to see him, to have someone to share these moments with. We chat for a while about plays we have been in, and it feels good, like old times. I notice Rory glance towards the door again.

'Am I keeping you?'

'It's a pain, but I do need to go and do my vocal warm-up.'

'This counts as a warm-up doesn't it? You can stay for another? I haven't seen you for ages.'

I realise I sound desperate again. Is Rory really the only person I have to hang out with? How has it got to this point? I used to have friends, didn't I? Maybe I should have stayed longer at the casting, invited the other actresses out for a drink. No, we are still in competition. Too awkward. Kim pops into my head. I could have invited her for a drink. OK, she works for me, but she was good at the casting, surprisingly so. But no, we aren't friends.

'I'm thinking of asking George to move out.' Am I? Well, it seems like a sure way to get Rory to listen, and stay a little longer.

Rory nearly spits out his whisky. 'What's prompted this? Is it because of the story about us? Is he still angry with you?' He looks concerned, which is sweet.

'It didn't help...' I study Rory's reaction.

Rory leans back in his chair. 'God, I thought that had all died down.'

Can I tell him about what it is really like, living with George? Rory will be surprised, worried about me. How will it feel to tell someone what is really going on? I notice him glance at the door a third time. He wants to leave. No, this isn't the time.

'I don't want to lose the house. It's mine,' I add.

Rory lets out a deep sigh and leans towards me. 'Did you do a pre-nup?'

I shake my head.

Rory exhales. 'Look, I'm no expert in this sort of thing. Let's talk about this when we've got more time. I need to get ready, get back to the theatre.' He drains his glass, and looks at me, concerned. 'Is it really that bad?'

'Oh, you know how it is. Just letting off steam. You need to get going.' I give Rory my best smile. He clearly doesn't want me to burden him.

He signals to the waiter. 'Let me get these, Jemima, honey.

Why don't you come and see the play, yes? It's a lot of fun. Cheer you up.'

'Sorry, are you Rory Jackson?' A woman touches him on the arm.

'Hi! Yes.'

'It is him!' She squeals to her friend, standing in her waterproof jacket by the door, hopelessly overdressed for the weather. He winks at me, and gets up for a selfie with the two women. God, he loves the attention.

My phone rings. Elle! I indicate that I will take the call, so Rory blows me a kiss and leaves, squeezing his way through the small crowd gathering in the doorway.

'Hi, Elle. How's things?' I ask, brightly.

'Jemima! You OK? How did the audition go?' The agency isn't far away, across Soho. Should I invite Elle to join me for a drink?

'Indira was there. And Kim. They are clearly not sure who they want, and what look. I mean, Elle, really... they know who I am. Did I really have to go through that? I'm hardly new at this game.' I realise that has come out a bit sharper than I have intended. This martini is strong.

Elle pauses for a moment, as if gathering her thoughts. 'Vikram actually called me, just now.'

Oh! Have they made a decision already? Suddenly, it all feels very real. I might actually have to do this. Can I learn a script of that length? I used to be able to be brilliant at learning lines, but it has been a while. What if I mess up, can't do it?

'Did he? What did he say?' I try to sound calm, in control.

'Vikram said that you didn't seem wholly committed to their casting process.'

What? 'That sounds like I'm being told off, Elle.' I feel anger start to rise up in me. 'I think Vikram has a rather inflated sense of himself.'

I see a large man turn around and look at me. Oh, sod off.

'Mmm. Yes, well, you know what these directors can be like. Dealing with their egos is all part of the game.'

Oh my god. Is Elle about to tell me that they turned me down? Is that what she is saying? That they don't want me? And implying it has been my fault. What sort of agent is she?

'You know Kim was auditioning at the same time as me? I honestly think you should have rung me, told me before. She is still working for me, and it was awkward. You put me in a very difficult position.'

I hear Elle take a deep breath. 'Kim's audition was quite last-minute. I do apologise for not letting you know. It is very busy in the office at the moment. That's why I'm calling, actually.'

'Go on...' I feel my stomach flip. Is she letting me go? That is unthinkable. I am too well-known.

'They are thinking of casting you and Kim together – as the sisters. How great is that?' Elle genuinely sounds excited at the prospect. 'We represent both of you, of course, so this would be quite something for the agency. But I wasn't sure how you'd feel about it all. It's a huge part for you, and it has been a while since you were on stage. Do you think you could manage? You can be totally honest with me.'

I sit there, trying to take it all in. They want me for the part! Not Indira. Or those other women. I am better than all of them. I feel my shoulders relax. I still have it, can still get the big parts.

But can I do it? Elle doesn't sound so sure. And she is right, it has been a long time since I have been on a stage, live, in front of all those people. No retakes. Nowhere to hide. And they want Kim as well. But she has barely acted...

'I can handle that script. I've done Chekov, for goodness' sake.'

The bartender picks up my empty glass and asks if I want another. I nod. Oh god, I've wanted to do a play, haven't I? But can I actually do it? The main part. And me, the name that everyone will come to see. The reason why people will buy tickets, the reason the critics will come. I feel my heart rate begin to speed up. I can still say no. I can still tell people I've got the part, and I've had to turn it down. But this is what I've trained for. When I was younger I would have killed for this chance.

'Jemima, you still there?' Elle asks, sounding a little worried.

'I am. Just thinking. It's a fantastic offer, thank you, Elle. Please do pass on my thanks to Vikram and Bill for asking me to do it—'

'Jemima, that sounds like you are going to turn it down,' Elle interrupts.

I pause, make sure she is concentrating. 'The thing is. It is a challenging part, for me. And you know, I've done so much TV recently, it has been a while since I stepped onto the stage. And in a lead role.'

'Yes. But this is why this is so perfect for you... get you back out there. We would all be supporting you.'

'Thank you, Elle. I appreciate that. But if this is going to work for me, then I need to have the right people around me.' I leave space for my words to sink in. 'I need to have experienced people around me. People I know will be great to work with.'

'Oh right.' Good. She is getting what I am saying.

'Kim is great, of course she is. But is she right for a play of this profile?' If I am going to do this play, I need Kim at home, helping me learn my lines and run the house when I am busy.

'Leoni says she is terrific. And if Bill and Vikram like her, then I really don't see why she couldn't do it. And they did say you look alike, which is such a positive.'

'Well, she didn't used to have red hair,' I remind her. I can't see the similarity myself. Men can be quite simple, sometimes. Same colour hair, and suddenly we look alike? Maybe in their eyes.'

'Can I tell them you are a yes? I am sure they will be thrilled to have you on board.' Elle wants to pin down her percentage.

'I need to review the contracts, though I'm sure you have got me a good deal.' Elle only gets paid if I do the work. She needs to remember who works for who, here.

'Of course! You know me,' Elle replies. 'I can send you over the contract. Give you time to think.'

'Great, thank you. And, Elle, shall I leave you to deal with the other matter?'

FIFTY-ONE

JEMIMA

'You almost ready, darling?'

Going to a screening is the very last thing I feel like doing. I need to read the contract and do some thinking. They will want a decision fast. Can I do this play?

'I can't. I need to decide. Elle says they are eager for me to do it. I think, maybe I should say yes...'

'Do you think it's a good idea?'

'Why wouldn't it be?'

'Oh, you know. Live theatre. Anything can go wrong. It's been a while since you did that.'

'You think it's too much?' I hate myself for asking him.

'Why put yourself through it? Filming is one thing, but live theatre? Best leave it to the youngsters.'

Why does he have to say it like that? 'The part is for my age.'

Maybe he's right though. What am I trying to prove? A younger Jemima would have jumped at this, but back then, I didn't have critics and online judgement to deal with. Back then, no one knew who I was.

'Get ready. Come on. I told people you'd be there.'

'I'm not in the mood, George. I need on focus on this.'

He rubs his hair, a sign of irritation I know only too well. 'I don't ask much from you, Jemima. This is important to me. You're meant to be my wife.'

He leans across me, and smacks my laptop shut.

FIFTY-TWO

KIM

You could cut the atmosphere with a knife. As soon as I closed the front door behind me, I knew something wasn't right. Low voices, tense. Jemima and George were in her office, George seemed to be speaking, but I couldn't make it out. I stood still for a second, and then called out, 'Hello?'

No reply, so I walked into the kitchen to stay out of the way. The kitchen island was covered in mess – dirty plates, coffee cups, used tissues. I started loading the dishwasher.

My lunch with Marianne had been so lovely – her flat-mates, Amy and Vicky, had joined us, too. They worked at theatres in the West End, and were so funny and kind, including me in their conversations, even though they had all known each other since college. It had been a long time since I had felt part of a friendship group, and I loved how the conver-sation ran over each other, as they completed each other's sentences, and yet they included me, and wanted to know all about me.

There was talk of Amy going on tour, and it crossed my mind that she might want someone to let her room when she was away, and that could even be me. But maybe it was too soon for that... I'd only just met them all, and really, I barely knew Marianne. Maybe one day. I felt a little jealous when they all piled into an Uber together to go back home, and I got the bus on my own. The front door banged, making me look round.

George appeared in the doorway.

'Thank you, Kim. You really shouldn't have to tidy up after Jemima.' He looked exhausted, poor thing.

'It's not a problem.'

He walked round the island and took a beer out of the fridge.

'You are such an asset here. I really appreciate it. We both do.' He took a swig from the bottle and wiped his mouth. 'Jemima says you auditioned for a part in her play. That's amazing.'

Her play. Well, it probably was going to be her play. They were bound to offer her the part as she was so well known.

'Yes, I'm not sure I will get this one. But I was pleased to be invited.'

'I remember when I was just starting out, never knowing if you would get it or not.' He pulled out a stool and sat down. He looked like he needed a friend. It would be mean to leave him here, drinking on his own. *When he finishes his beer, I'll head downstairs.*

'Did you do many plays? Or was it always films for you?'

George smiled, his face creasing. 'Loads when I was at drama school, then the early years. Always played the villain though.' He laughed. 'I don't have the face to play the leading man.'

I flushed. 'Oh... I'm sure that's not true. Do you miss it?'

'The stage? No, I'm more than happy in film. Easier. And better money. But there's nothing like being in front of a live audience. That feeling of anything can happen, the adrenaline of it.' He took another swig of beer, and looked at me, his expression serious. 'Between you and me, I do worry about Jemima. This play... well, it will be very challenging for her. She hasn't done a live performance for quite a while.'

I found myself nodding, not sure what to say in response. Had she got the part then? If she'd found out already, did that mean I was a no? I felt my heart sink.

'She's already stressed about it, and it hasn't even started yet,' he said, rubbing his head.

'I'm sorry to hear that.' So, yes, that sounded like Jemima had got the play. She hadn't even told me. I had started to think that yes, just maybe, I was in with a chance. But no. What was I thinking? I wasn't an actor. I was just pretending.

'I'm due to go out in a minute. A screening of my friend's film. I hate those things. You have to say how much you love it, no matter how bad it is. Tepo is a great friend though. I really should show my face.'

I stared at him. 'Not Tepo Din? The director? You know him? I've seen loads of his films!'

'You are very sweet. I fear his best work might be behind him.' George stood up, and placed his bottle into the recycling. 'Come if you want? I'm leaving soon. Shame to waste the extra ticket. And there will be delicious warm white wine, of course.'

'Oh, I couldn't possibly...'

I paused. Did he mean it? It would be so cool to go to a film screening. *Who knows who I might meet there?* And it would take my mind off the inevitable rejection from the play that was coming my way. If I stayed here, I'd only be lying on the sofa in the basement, feeling sorry for myself.

'Doesn't Jemima want to go?'

George shook his head. 'Seriously, you'd be doing me a favour. If Tepo comes over to talk to me, you say something nice, and he will be so distracted by you, I won't have to say anything.' He grinned. 'Probably best to be out of the house when Jemima gets home. She's in one of her moods.' He walked over to the door. 'Can you be ready in ten?' He paused, and looked at me, smiling.

'Sure! Thanks. I'd love to come.'

'Great! You are doing me a favour. And, Kim? If you want my advice, wear that green dress. It really suits you.'

FIFTY-THREE

KIM

'You look incredible.' George appeared in the hallway, wearing a navy jacket that made him look younger, somehow.

'Are you really sure Jemima doesn't want to go?' I asked, trying not to stare too much.

'No idea when she'll be back. She hates this sort of thing. Anything to do with my old friends bores her silly.'

The journey flew by, with us sat together in the back, chatting about films, things we'd seen and loved. I was almost sad when we stopped behind the concrete building that was home to the British Film Institute. George leapt out and opened the car door for me. I followed him towards the river. I loved being on the Southbank – there was a magical energy about the place, with such a cross-section of London life going about their day – the street performers, theatregoers, tourists, boats going past, the London Eye turning in the distance.

A red carpet and ropes had been set up outside the BFI, and we walked in, past the people drinking at outdoor tables. One woman glanced up at me as I walked past, checking to see if she knew me. *Not yet, lady, but watch this space.*

Inside, the place was painted blood red – it was like walking into a seedy nightclub. I'd never been in here before, though I'd walked past many times. A waiter held out a tray of drinks. That could have been me, doing that job, but here I was, a guest, and with a famous actor by my side. It was amazing how much had changed since I had started working for the Edens.

'George!' A cheery looking man, dressed in an excellent vintage suit, came over and slapped George on the arm.

'Howard! Amazing to see you.' George pulled the man into a warm hug.

'No Jemima this evening? Gone for a younger model?' I could feel Howard's eyes skim my body.

George laughed. 'This is Kim. Family friend. Actor and film buff. And apparently Tepo's biggest fan.'

'Excellent! See you both for a drink after.'

'Stay very clear of him. He has quite the reputation,' George whispered.

George seemed to know everyone, stopping to talk several times, before we found two seats near the front. As I sat down, trying not to crease my dress, I felt George's arm around my shoulder, as if helping me into place. I glanced around, wondering if anyone was watching us. George moved a little closer, his arm resting gently against mine.

And there he was! Tepo Din, the award-winning film director. He strode onto the stage and introduced his film, explaining the inspiration behind it. George leaned in, his warm breath on my cheek. 'I'll introduce you afterwards.'

I nodded, and smiled in the darkness.

The house was very quiet when we got back. The after-party had gone on until late, and it had been a blur of celebrities and influential people, and George seemed to know them all. He was incredibly generous, introducing me to people he had worked with, telling everyone that I was an actor. I couldn't fail to notice the occasional raised eyebrow from the middle-aged men, clearly wondering why *I* was there with George rather than Jemima, but he seemed unfazed by that. And as promised, he introduced me to the director, Tepo Din, and I was pleased I didn't sound like an idiot, and managed to say how much I loved the film. *If Mum could see me now!*

'Thank you for tonight,' I said to George as he threw his jacket over the banister. It felt awkward standing there, the two of us, with Jemima sleeping somewhere above us. *I should leave now. Go down to the basement. End the evening here.* But something compelled me to stay.

'You are so welcome. It is lovely to be with someone who appreciates all this. It's easy to get jaded when you've been in this business such a long time. Nightcap?'

The last thing I needed was more alcohol, but I found myself following him into the kitchen. I watched him pour out two large whiskies.

'So, what did you really think of the film?' I asked, trying to keep the conversation light.

'Hated it! He's trying too hard to make something worthy, you know? Just give us what we want – quirky, interesting. Doesn't have to be deep. You were brilliant though, Kim. Charmed Tepo. You really were the perfect guest.'

'Thank you.' I took a sip of the whisky, and felt it warm my throat.

'We used to be like this,' George said, taking a sip of his drink. 'When we first dated. Going to screenings, first nights. It was a lot of fun.'

'You and Jemima?' I asked, a little stupidly. Who else could he mean? George nodded.

'Yes. Good times. Don't ever change, Kim. Stay exactly as you are.' Sitting there, in the low lighting of the kitchen, he looked sad, a little lost. Not many people saw him like this –

most saw him as he was tonight at the party – confident, owning the room. We're all actors, really, aren't we?

George stood up, placed his glass down, and took a step towards me. He placed his warm hand on my arm, then leaned towards me. Oh god, was he going to kiss me?

I felt my face turn towards his, instinctive, expectant.

He hesitated, as if deciding what to do, his lips so close to mine... and then he pulled me towards him, into a hug, firm and confident. I could feel the bristles of his evening shadow on my face, and the heat coming from his body. I felt my body relax into his. And then it was over, and he stepped back.

'Goodnight, Kim.' And then he left me, to go and join Jemima in bed.

FIFTY-FOUR

KIM

When Leoni called me I nearly fell off the sofa in my rush to answer the call. My heart pounding, I pressed answer.

'Hello?'

'Kim. How are you? OK? I've got amazing news!'

Oh my god, oh my god. I got the part! I'm going to be in a London play! I couldn't believe how far my life had changed in the last couple of months. Taking this job had turned my life around. I realised I needed to reply.

'Hi, Leoni. Hi. Thanks so much!'

'Vikram called and they want to cast you in the play. You will be the understudy for the two sisters. Isn't that great!'

Understudy? I swallowed. Oh right. I hadn't thought about that. Of course they needed an understudy. Which is why they had seen me. What was I thinking? I was so unknown, they weren't going to give me a main part. Especially playing alongside someone as famous as Jemima Eden. What an idiot.

'That's great! Thanks so much, Leoni. What does that involve?' I asked, trying to sound enthusiastic.

'I'm so pleased you're pleased! I do enjoy these moments of my job. It's a great opportunity. You get to learn both parts, go to all the rehearsals, and of course, you need to be at the theatre every show, just in case you are needed to step in on the night.'

'Does that happen very much?' *So, I might do all that work and then never get to actually go on stage? Is that what she's saying?*

I could practically hear Leoni working out what to say. 'Well, it is a short run, so the chances of being on stage are lower than, say if you were doing a long-running West End musical. But you never know. Actors do get ill. It's all part of it. And you will learn so much just by being there, with such a great team. It all goes on your CV, of course. And it pays fairly well. And you get more if you actually perform, did you know that?'

'I didn't.'

'I'll send the paperwork through. And the good thing is, Jemima is delighted! Says you can carry on working for her, and do the play at the same time, so I hope that works for you?'

She'd spoken to Jemima about this, before me? Of course she had. Jemima Eden was one of the agency's most important clients. There was no way they would offer this to me without her approval. Maybe Jemima had put in a good word for me, had got me this role? Or George, even. I had a very strong feeling that there were decisions being made above me.

'It's a yes, Kim, isn't it?' Leoni was still talking.

I had to take it. I'd be crazy to turn it down. It was good experience, she was right. The disappointment of not getting one of the main parts would soon leave me. This was a positive step in the right direction. More money, so that was something. And maybe I would get to go on stage.

'Thanks so much, Leoni. You're the best.'

FIFTY-FIVE

JEMIMA

Oh god, why did I agree to do this stupid play? Elle has sent through a schedule of rehearsal and performance dates. The Soho Place marketing team were in touch as soon as I signed the contract – they wanted to set up a photoshoot so they could make posters and get started on their marketing campaign, and it was clear that I was at the heart of that. Each time I pick up the script, I feel anxious.

George has flown out to Budapest for a project, which has given me some much-needed headspace. He has texted a few times already, to check how I'm getting on, which isn't helping. Kim is being great, helping me organise everything. She has made a colourful planner which is now stuck on my office door, showing which days I need to be at the theatre, when I have wardrobe, marketing, press... The single date in highlighted in red caught my eye. Opening night. It looks far too soon.

My phone rings. Elle. She's been in constant touch these past few days.

'Jemima! Morning! The production team messaged to ask if you are OK to do some TV promo? Panel shows, that sort of thing. I said a tentative yes, of course.'

Live TV? This was all getting too much. 'We haven't even started rehearsals, Elle. This is going too fast.' I sound panicky, unprofessional.

'Oh, it will be in couple of weeks. Ages yet. You will be well into the flow of rehearsals by then. You know how these things work – they like to book celebs ahead.'

'I'm not sure I'll have time.'

I can hear Elle choose her words carefully. 'You'll be fine, Jemima. Just one or two interviews should be enough. I'll ask for the questions in advance. It's so important for your profile, too, not just the play.'

It's easy for her to say, it's not her being watched, judged. What if the play isn't good? We've barely begun. At least Sam McKinnon, the man playing my husband, is good. I've watched him in a few episodes of a crime drama he's been in. And I knew Kim of course.

Ah yes. I need to update you on that. Kim. I've been quite clever there. George had pointed out that Kim leaving now would be inconvenient for me. She might get a part somewhere else, and then I'd be without anyone to help me. So, I'd rung Elle and said I had a suggestion. What if, I said, Kim could be an understudy in the play? She could cover the younger sister part. She'd be working at the theatre, but she wouldn't actually be that busy. She would still be able to work for me at home. Perfect!

Kim was absolutely adorable when she found out, and came in to the office right after she'd heard, grinning from ear to ear. It crossed my mind that I was the first person she told. Funny how she never really mentions any family. I wonder what the story is there...

I made it very clear to Kim that I needed her to help me as a priority, and she'd been completely fine with that. And rightly so, as she wouldn't have this important understudy position if she didn't know me. I'm helping her into the industry. It takes me back to when I was starting out. It would have been amazing if someone had stepped up to help me, but I very much had to make it on my own.

I suggested Kim stay here, on rehearsal days, if we've had a late night, and she was delighted with that. Just a short-term thing, of course.

Kim is so grateful; it really is ideal. She's fine for us to rehearse late, as often as I want, and she's incredibly patient, going over tricky passages until I get them right. Scene two in particular, is tough – so repetitive. I'm determined to know most of the script before the first full rehearsal. As the lead actor it's all on me to set the tone, to be the best in the room, the most professional.

Honestly, I recommend living with a fellow actor! You can get so much done. And I have to say, she is quite good. I mean, she's just reading the lines, really at this point, but I can see that she would be good in the sister part, if she ever does need to step in. I can't imagine Sarah will miss many shows though – she is such a pro, and so perfect for the part. Apparently, Vikram and Bill were considering Kim very seriously for the role, but I did say to Elle that I thought it was too soon, and she lacked the experience, and it was good that they listened to me.

My mind keeps taking me back to filming in Scotland, and when I had got the lines wrong. But I had taken a break before then, so no wonder I had been rusty. I will be amazing in this. Everyone will see that.

First full rehearsal today. I should do some breathing exercises, calm down. It's just a rehearsal! It will be good for me to get out of the house more, to get back to what I do best. I've been hiding away here, for far too long.

Kim texts.

Car here. I've packed lunch and snacks for us both X

Ending with the kiss is a little too familiar, but I can forgive her that. I look at my carefully annotated script, curling a little at the edges now from all the read-throughs. I take a deep breath. I want this, don't I?

FIFTY-SIX

KIM

'It's a nightmare,' I told Marianne as she handed me a large glass of wine.

'She's known for being a diva. You have my sympathy.'

Rehearsals had started well, with everyone on their best behaviour. The directors, Bill and Vikram, had sat us all in a circle and introduced us all, and it felt surreal to be there, among so many well-known people. The first read-through had been with the scripts in our hands, and that was fun as you could see the play start to come to life, with all the different voices. It was so much more interesting than just reading it in your head. I didn't get to read, of course, just being the under-study, but I sat near Jemima, and listened. Jemima had charmed the room, handing out brownies I had made earlier.

It was when the cast had to try scenes without the scripts that it had gone pear-shaped. Jemima knew her words – we had gone over them so many times, and she was almost word-perfect at home, but here it was very different. I could see Bill and Vikram exchange glances, as they had to start a scene again. I could tell Jemima was getting tense, her earlier enthusiasm fast evaporating.

I took a sip of wine. This was delicious and expensive. 'It's early days. I shouldn't be a bitch. This helps, thanks,' I said to Marianne. She was working on a daytime quiz show, which she hated, but it clearly paid OK.

My phone buzzed. *George.* George was texting me. He had flown to Budapest for work. We hadn't spoken much since the film party; there was so much going on, and it seemed like Jemima was always around. It was all go on *Mosquitoes*, and Jemima and I had a full schedule of rehearsals, and he'd been busy, too.

I had to say, it was much calmer in the house with George away. Jemima seemed happier, too. She was downstairs more often, and was quite chatty with me in the mornings, and even made me coffee yesterday. That might also be excitement for being in the play, of course. It was sweet of Jemima to say I could use a spare room sometimes. She told me to use the room at the far end of the corridor, easily the smallest of their many bedrooms, but it suited me just fine, for now. I still used the basement as my office though – it was too far to come up here in the day. I felt strangely attached to it.

> How's it going? How are my two favourite actresses?

If he wanted to know how Jemima was getting on, surely he should just ask her?

'Secret admirer?' Marianne asked, smiling at me.

I shook my head. 'Work thing.'

> Great! All going well.

I put my phone face-down.

'So, are you loving it? Being in the play? I can't wait to see it.' Marianne and some of the Scottish crew had already booked tickets for the opening night, which was so lovely of them. I felt

I should have tried to get them comps, but I had no idea how to do that. As an understudy, did I even get free tickets? I wasn't sure.

'It's OK. The directors seem pleased with me. I'm enjoying it, rehearsing. I've not done that much yet, just run my lines with the assistant director and the male understudy. I might get to do it with the main actors soon, when they feel more ready. Apparently, they don't want to confuse anyone – I think they mean Jemima really. It's OK, that's being an understudy... though, really, I should be getting to run it through by now with the main cast.'

'I see.' Marianne nodded.

'Vikram said I might have a small walk-on part, just playing someone in the background, but at least I will get to be on stage! They're still working that bit out.'

'That would be so cool! You'll get a costume and everything!'

Well, yes, hopefully. The reality was I'd only been told to try on Sarah's and Jemima's costumes. Wardrobe didn't make new costumes just for the understudy. Luckily, Jemima and I were about the same size. Sarah a little smaller, but I would manage.

I took another swallow of wine. 'Only downside is, I don't get to switch off. When I get back to the house, Jemima wants to run lines, or talk about the day.' That involved her mostly complaining about something the directors had told her to do. She took it as criticism, but mostly it was just direction, and the rest of the actors just got on with it. We had been meant to finish at six yesterday, but Jemima had insisted they try a scene in the way she wanted, and it was a late night for everyone. I could see the glances exchanged between the other actors, as they had to do it again, her way.

'Maybe you should move in with us? She sounds like she's taking advantage of you,' Marianne said kindly.

'Thanks. I think I just need to get to opening night, make sure Jemima is OK, and then, yes, let's talk about that.' An image of George, smiling at me in the kitchen appeared in my head. I wasn't sure I was ready to leave that house, just yet.

'You are too good to her. Jemima sounds exhausting.'

I nodded. But I knew that if I could help Jemima, then ultimately it would be good for the play. And who knows, it might get extended, I might get to go on stage and someone important might see me. Any night, there could be a casting agent in the audience, or a director, and I could be discovered, and get another part. And once the play was going well, I could move out. It was all so close – a dream life. I was working as an actor. I had an agent who was finding me these opportunities. I had friends. I wish I could tell Mum all about it. She would have been there on opening night for sure, probably right in the centre of the front row, as proud as anything.

It was getting late, and we had an early start for rehearsals in the morning. I drained my glass. 'One more? Before I head back? My round.' I did feel more relaxed. It felt so good to be able to talk all this through with someone.

'You sit there! Sounds like you had a tough day. I'll get them.' Marianne grabbed our empty glasses, and went over to the bar.

My phone pinged. George again.

Great! Glad it's going well.

I replied.

Rehearsals are a bit intense. Hard work!!

I could see Marianne coming back already, with two very large glasses of wine.

I bet you're amazing.

I stared at the phone. What was I meant to say to that?

FIFTY-SEVEN

JEMIMA

Opening night is just three days away and we are not ready. I told the directors that we should consider delaying the opening by a week at least, but they were incredibly rude to me about it. I've sent Kim out for cigarettes. George wouldn't approve, but then, he isn't here to judge me, is he? I call Elle. She'll know what to do.

'Honestly, Elle. It would be better to delay the opening, and get it right! They could just say there are technical issues.'

'I've spoken to Vikram, Jemima. He says you're ready. Opening night will be fine – it's mostly an invited crowd anyway. They're all on your side.'

'Critics are never on your side. They love it if they can find something negative to say.'

I exhale loudly. Critics will be eager to get the knives out, to say I was terrible, that I should have stayed in TV, had no right to be on stage. What was I thinking, taking this on? I'm a complete idiot; I've brought this on myself.

'They might love it, Jemima. Don't be so negative.' What the hell does Elle know? George is right. This is a mistake.

'I can't do it, Elle.'

'Jemima, listen. Honestly, this is such a normal reaction to opening night. It's just nerves.'

'Nerves... You have no idea. You've never been in this position.'

Elle went very quiet. Oh hell, why had I said that? She told me years ago that she trained as an actor, but had switched to becoming an agent very early on. I swallow. 'Sorry, I'm stressed.'

'Listen, you'll be great, Jemima. You know the part. You've worked incredibly hard. I know you'll be good. Just try and stay calm this week. Get out for some walks. Get some sleep. All that good stuff.'

Like it was that easy. I glance at the kitchen clock. I will need to leave soon for dress rehearsal. That's another issue. My costume is incredibly uncomfortable. God knows what it will feel like under hot stage lights.

'Leoni and I will be there on Friday to cheer you on. George is aiming to be back, too, isn't he? Honestly Jemima, don't worry. We're all rooting for you.'

George is due to fly back late on Friday afternoon. I close my eyes at the thought. Something had to change there. It's been so peaceful without him here. I sigh. 'OK, Elle. Listen, I'm going to go. Car will be here soon.'

'Atta girl. I'll pop in and see you in your dressing room on opening night, if you like? Before you go on?'

'No, don't do that. I'll be nervous enough.'

I hear Elle sigh. 'OK. All good! See you Friday, Jemima. Call me if you need anything. Any time.'

FIFTY-EIGHT

KIM

It's almost opening night. For the past few days we had been at the theatre early and stayed until late. Jemima was off doing something with the costume people, so Vikram suggested we take the time for me to run through her part, just in case I was ever needed to understudy Jemima. I felt less sure about the older sister role. I needed to have a more serious tone, change my posture, act like I was a scientist. I tried to think about how Jemima did it. How she stood. How she used her voice.

The lines came easily, well, of course they did – I had run them with Jemima so many times. I just switched into her role and got on with it, imagining myself as her. I noticed Sam, playing my husband, smile. Relief that I could do it? I could almost see the other actors relax, as we worked our way through the scenes, and each one went smoothly. We got to the end of scene two, and I'd got it word perfect. I looked across at Vikram. *Nailed it.* Now everyone knew I would be OK if I was ever needed. I was ready.

. . .

Our car swooshed through the rainy streets on the way to the theatre. It would have been faster to get the tube in this weather, but that wasn't Jemima Eden's style. Blacked-out windows meant that I could watch people going about their busy lives, but they couldn't see us. I wonder what they would think to know that the famous Jemima Eden was sitting here in this car. This morning Jemima had seemed tense, subdued. I tried to be reassuring, but she barely looked at me.

'Pull over here, please, John.' I was surprised when Jemima spoke. We pulled up outside a shop with crates of fruit and vegetables outside. Jemima looked so out of place, in her black coat and sunglasses, among the market shoppers and boxes of rubbish. Moments later, she was back in the car with a large bag of oranges.

'An old teacher of mine always bought oranges for us, ahead of a show, to boost our immune systems,' she explained.

'That's a lovely idea,' I replied, a little surprised.

When we got to the rehearsal, she handed the oranges out to everyone, including the production crew. I saw Vikram and Bill glance at each other. None of us were used to this Jemima. I could see she was trying to be upbeat, positive, but I knew her better than most – the creases on her face showed she had barely slept.

The dress rehearsal went well. Jemima needed prompting a few times, but it was OK. She even thanked Vikram for a last-minute stage direction, nodding, and agreeing that, 'Yes, that is better, thank you.'

In the car home that night, she asked me to run through the first scene lines again.

'Of course.'

Jemima reached into her bag to get her script out.

'You've got this. Don't use your script,' I said, and instantly regretted it.

'That's my call, not yours,' Jemima shot back.

I turned to her. 'You know your lines. Honestly, you don't need your script now.'

'Oh, it's OK for you to say that. No one is coming to watch you in this.'

I sat back, stunned. So, back to the old Jemima. What was I meant to say to that? Right then, I wished I had made my own way back, wasn't stuck here, dealing with this. I did have friends coming to watch me, actually, even if I was only on stage for a brief moment. Did she? Did she have any actual friends at all? Not that I knew of.

I glanced at her, leaning back in her seat, staring out of the window. She looked so alone, lost in her thoughts. So, I was meant to comfort her, was that it? The rich, privileged actress who had it all. Is this what she paid me for, to soothe her fragile ego? Well, soon I'd be able to quit this job. I would be paid soon for the play, and then I would be able to cover the rent at Marianne's, and move on with my life. But I also really needed this play to work and that meant not pissing off Jemima. I took a deep breath.

'You're going to be amazing. You've got this! And yes, you're right... people are coming to see you. And they are going to love it. They are going to love *you*.'

She turned to look at me. 'You really think so?'

'I do.'

Jemima leaned back against the headrest. 'It's going to work, isn't it?' There was such a sense of relief in her voice.

'It's going to be brilliant,' I replied, and right then, in that moment, I believed it.

'You've been great, Kim. Really. I know it's not always been easy working for me, but I... well, I couldn't have done this without you.' She glanced at me, just for a second.

'I wouldn't even be here without you,' I replied. And that was true. If I hadn't gone to work for Jemima Eden, I wouldn't have got my agent and be in this play. I owed her a lot.

'We make a good team,' she replied.

That night she made me a cup of her special herbal tea ('good for our voices') before she said goodnight. I couldn't tell her yet that I was leaving, but I would, as soon as opening night was out of the way, and the play was going smoothly. She wouldn't need me then, and I wouldn't need her.

FIFTY-NINE

KIM

'Kim!' Jemima came charging into her office, still wearing her dressing gown. 'You seen this? Do you know anything about this?'

She held out her phone, right in my face. A news website. A photo of Jemima and Rory having a drink in a cosy bar. She scrolled down. Another photo, this time of them walking in a park together. The headline shouted:

Jemima's sexy co-star!

Ahead of her opening night in the sparkling West End, Jemima Eden gets cosy with Dragonhunter star, Rory Jackson.

'Look! There are loads of shitty comments.' I stared at the screen. It had been weeks since the last rumours of Jemima and Rory had come out. Did she think this was *me*?

'It must be because it's opening night.' I looked at her. 'They're just running the same story...'

'That one in the bar is a new photo. We only went for one drink! This sounds like we are in the same play – it's so stupid. I bet it was the barman who took this. After some easy money. Look what they are saying about me in the comments! So nasty... George will go crazy.'

This was the last thing we needed on opening night. Jemima looked so stressed. This wouldn't help her concentrate. 'Have you spoken to Elle?'

Jemima shook her head. 'I've left messages, but she hasn't got back to me.'

'It is early still. I'm sure she will.' I watched her pace across the room.

'Oh god. What will Vikram and Bill say? And the rest of the cast? This is now all about me. It's not meant to be like that. It's meant to be a company, a team...'

Was this bad news for the play? No publicity is bad publicity, right? But then, if Jemima was freaking out, she could really mess up tonight. And it was me here, dealing with her.

'Let me get you something to eat. You get dressed. Elle will know what to do.'

I was making smoothies when Jemima came running into the kitchen. 'Vikram messaged me. Look. He sounds angry, doesn't he?'

I read the text message on her phone.

Not great. Come in early for a chat.

'What does he want a meeting for?' she asked me, panic in her eyes.

'Maybe just to check you're OK? Why don't you call him?'

'I've tried. Went to voicemail. Probably avoiding the press. Oh, this is such a mess.'

I needed to rescue this, calm her down. 'Look. Drink this. You are going to need your energy today.'

'I'm not sure I can eat anything right now, Kim,' she snapped. 'I'm not even sure I can go on tonight. They will all be gossiping about me. No one will be interested in the play. It will all be about my personal life.'

I heard a car door slam outside. Journalists?

'I need to call Rory.'

'Is that a good idea?' I looked at her. Was it true, then, that she had been having an affair? The photos did look pretty damning... and there was that day in the spa. But in all the time I had been working for her, she so rarely went out at all. And during rehearsals, she had been far too busy, surely? Oh, what would poor George think? He was due to fly in later. He would be devastated.

'Rory's not picking up either,' Jemima said, staring at her phone.

'Probably thinks it's a journalist or something.'

'He has my number! Are we going to have the press camped up outside again?' She walked over to the window and looked out. 'Oh god, who are they?'

'Maybe we should go to the theatre. Better than staying here. You can see Vikram.'

She turned to look at me. 'The press will be at the theatre, too, won't they? Trying to get photos of me.'

I needed to calm her down. *Think, Kim. What can I say that will make her feel better?* My phone buzzed. Marianne.

Saw the news. You OK?

She was up early. I glanced at the kitchen clock. It was going to be a very long day.

'Who's that?' Jemima demanded.

'Just a friend.'

I replied:

It's nothing. Old news.

On your opening night!! Your diva boss
probably planned it. See you tonight. Can't wait
to see you. Star!!!

I sent a thumbs up and then deleted the message. Couldn't risk Jemima seeing anyone calling her a diva. People were coming to see me tonight. The show *would* happen... wouldn't it?

Jemima was reading her phone. I hoped she wasn't looking at her socials. No good could come of that. I would need to go through and delete as many toxic comments as I could. *Had* she planted the story herself? It didn't seem at all likely. She was so upset. Clearly, it had been a shock for her.

I took my smoothie over to the window and sat still, trying to think. It wasn't like Marianne to text so early. She usually worked so late, she was more of a night owl. I looked at Jemima, so anxious, hunched over her phone. And then it hit me, with a sickening clarity. I had sat with Marianne, over drinks, and I had talked about Jemima. What had I said? Had I said anything about Rory? Maybe when we were up in Scotland. But nothing I shouldn't have...

Newspapers paid for stories, didn't they? What if they had paid *Marianne*? And I'd given her the information. I hadn't known Marianne that long. How well did I really know her? I realised, with a sinking heart, that I didn't know her at all. What if Jemima found out?

Softly, I spoke to Jemima. 'Maybe you should come off your phone. It won't help.'

'I need to know what they are saying about me.' She looked so vulnerable, face drawn from lack of sleep.

'Do you? Right now, you need to focus on tonight. Ignore all this. Focus on the play.' I badly needed to salvage this situation, get Jemima back on track. 'You've worked so hard for this. Don't let this take it away from you.'

And then Jemima did something that really shocked me. She walked across the kitchen, and pulled me into a hug. I felt her body against mine, and we sat there, for just a few seconds, united.

'Thank you for being here with me, Kim. It's nice to have someone on my side.'

She pulled back, and I looked at her. It felt like I was seeing the real Jemima. Scared, vulnerable and, for just a split second, real. Jemima's phone rang, breaking the spell.

'Elle! At last.' Jemima turned away from me and walked over to the island. 'So glad you called me. It's a bloody nightmare. Yes, I'm at home. So, what do I do?'

I busied myself taking lunch out of the fridge, trying to look like I wasn't listening in.

SIXTY

JEMIMA

Elle tried to calm me down. 'Rise above it, Jemima. You've dealt with this all before. We should have expected it really. Those hacks will use anything for clickbait. Don't let them ruin your day.'

She's right. I've worked so hard to get to this point, and this is a big day for me. I can't let a few photos and some stupid rumours spoil it for me. If only I could stop my body from shaking. I need to pull it together if I'm going to go on stage tonight.

Kim has gone to get her stuff together, ready to leave. It's nice having her here, in many ways, helping things run smoothly. I make a pot of tea, spooning the leaves into my teapot, pouring over the just-boiling water, and take a cup to the window seat. The heat of the mug begins to warm my hands. *Breathe in, Jemima.* I take a sip of the soothing liquid, and feel my shoulders relax. *Focus on one thing at a time. Drink your tea, then get in the car, and then deal with whatever happens next.*

There are raised voices outside. I look across the lawn and see two men standing just beyond the front gate. They're in dark coats, the hoods pulled up. Journalists.

I jump up and walked away from the window, standing

where I know no one can look in. What do they expect to see? Me, in floods of tears? Rory running up the path, into my arms? Idiots. Well, they can stand out there in the rain if they want. The most they'll get is a shot of me and Kim getting in the car to go to the theatre.

I need to keep calm before tonight, act like this is all OK. I've dealt with worse in the past. Now, where is Kim? We should go.

What was that? A car horn. Shouting. I walk closer to the window and peered out. The journalists are arguing with each other... no, with someone else. George! I watch him push one man, making him stumble back, clearly shouting at him, telling him to go, and then he's walking fast up the path towards the front door.

'Jemima! Where are you?' The front door slams as George storms into the hallway.

'You're back early—' I manage. Outside, I can hear the men swearing, shouting. One of them walking up the path.

George crashes into the kitchen, throwing his bag on the floor. 'Got the first flight. Those fuckers outside... I told them where to shove their cameras.'

I try to stay calm. 'You saw the news.'

'Yes.'

'We're going soon. Kim and I. The car is coming in a minute.'

George run his hands over his head. I didn't like that expression. I know it only too well.

'You must have been up early to get here now?' I glance at the kitchen clock. *Oh god*, I hope Kim had booked the car to come soon.

'I barely slept. I booked the first flight back.'

When did he see the story? Last night?

George walks over to the coffee machine and pulls out an espresso cup. As the machine hisses into life he turns to look at me. 'This is madness, Jemima. You doing this play. It's brought this press attention back on us.'

'But you know what they're saying isn't true. Rory is just a friend.' And George does know that. Rory and I have always been friends. He isn't even into women, though he doesn't want the press to know that. Doesn't suit the image he wants to portray, the leading man, a romantic hero. 'You know I'm not his type,' I remind George.

He shrugs. 'So he says. He'd say anything to get what he wants. I know men like him. He just uses you, for your name. Honestly, Jemima, you are so desperate for friends, you can't see it.'

I tried to control my breathing. How dare he say that.

'George. Everyone knows Rory is gay. Well, everyone in the business, anyway. Your friends... anyone that matters.'

He lets out a deep sigh. 'But clearly the press don't. People out there. Who go to my films. It makes me look like a fool. And I'm not—'

'I know that...' I reply. 'You're tired. Me too. This will all pass. We made the story go away last time, and we can do that again.'

The key here is to stay calm, not escalate things.

'Darling, look, I need to go to the theatre. Vikram wants to see me. To decide how to handle this.'

George stares. 'You're going there, now? Leaving me to deal with this?'

'You don't have to do anything. Just ignore them. Get some rest.' He could do with a shower – he looks crumpled and sweaty from the early flight. That would make him feel better, too.

George shakes his head. 'No. This needs to stop. You can't go to the theatre. Not today.'

'It's opening night, George. I have to go.' I swallow.

'No, Jemima. You aren't listening to me. Stop. All this. Your stupid play. You don't even need to do it. You've got nothing to prove.'

'It's not a stupid play, George. I want to do it. It's been too long... It's what I'm good at.'

He shakes his head. 'We don't need it. We've got all this.' He waves his hands around, indicating the kitchen, our house, our wealth.

'I need to go George. They need me there, at the theatre.' I smile at him. 'You are so kind, I know you want the best for me, but I'll be OK.'

Even while I back towards the door, I try to soothe George. 'I really appreciate you coming home early. I'll call you when I get there, let you know I'm OK, yes?'

He reaches out, and takes hold of my arm, pulling me into him. 'No. You need to stay here. You're not listening to me, Jemima.'

I look down at his hand. 'George, you're hurting me.' I try to pull away. Up close, I can smell the coffee on his breath, mixed with something else, something alcoholic.

'You need to pull out of the play.'

I stare at him. 'What are you talking about?'

'I've had enough, Jemima. Of all of it. You, wanting fame, to be admired by everyone. You should only want me! I thought this would make you stop. Give it up.' He tries to pull me towards him, into a hug, his arms too tight around my shoulders, my neck. I wriggle back, try to pull away, but he holds me close.

'You know I want a child... a family. And yet, here you are, still chasing fame. It's all about you! All the time. How can we bring a child into this world when you never have time for anything else?'

What is he even talking about? What does he mean, *I thought this would make you stop?*

His mouth is so close to my ear. 'Let Kim do it. Take your

part. She's the understudy, right? You don't need to do this. Just tell them you can't. That the press intrusion is too much.'

I pull myself away and stumble towards the door. Gulping in air, I stammer, 'Wait... was it you who sold the story? The men out there... are you trying to sabotage my career?'

'It was to *help* you! You are your own worst enemy, Jemima. Always chasing the next thing, when you should be here, with me. Raising our family.'

I feel the blood rush to my head. 'Our family? What family? We lost her.'

A black-and-white grainy image comes into my mind. The profile of a face, a round belly, tiny feet, hands... I'd wanted her so badly, but she was too good for this world. She hadn't wanted to come here. Had wanted to stay right there, safe in my body. It had been two years ago, and I thought about her every single day.

'Your work did this to us. If you had stopped working, she might still be alive.'

His words cut into me like a blade. 'It wasn't my fault—'

'You put your *career* first. Fame. And you didn't keep her safe.'

I stare at him. I had wanted her so much. The grief had kept me here for years, not working, not going out. He knows that better than anyone.

'I tried, George! You know I did. Every month I willed it to happen.'

And it had happened, at least twice. The early morning sickness, the ache in my breasts, but then the bleeding... the emptiness.

'You're blaming me?' I ask. What else did he want from me? He wanted me to stay forever at home, stop working, only focus on getting pregnant again? Like I hadn't tried? Maybe you only get so much luck in life, and I didn't get to be an actor and a mother. And this was my punishment, to live in this house, with all these beautiful rooms, so ready to be filled with children, but forever just us. Perhaps I did deserve this.

'I'm sorry, George, but we both know that isn't our story. I wanted children. So much. But this? You calling the press? Trying to control me. That's madness.'

I edge towards the kitchen door, trying to act calm. People are expecting me. I need to be at the theatre; that's where I'm needed, where I belong. I'd stayed here in this house with George for far too long, holding on to the memory of what we'd once had.

'It's over, George. We both know that.'

George is behind me in seconds, and slams the kitchen door shut.

'No. You don't get to decide that.'

I feel myself being pulled backwards, and the room tips around me as I hit the floor. Stunned, I lie there for a second. I can feel the hard cold of the kitchen tiles beneath my hands as I tried to push myself up. And then George is towering over me. His hand grabs my arm, as if he's going to help me up, and I reach up to him. A sharp, painful sting across my face. He's slapped me! Adrenaline floods through my body and I try once more to stand up, but the blows keep coming. There's a loud ringing in my ears, as blood rushes into my head. I feel dizzy, disoriented; the floor underneath me is moving, sliding away. Hot breath, near my face. A ringing sound, loud, persistent. Is the ringing inside my head, or a phone, somewhere in the distance...?

George is shouting at me, something about me being so self-ish, ruining everything...

I will myself to get up and away from him. I try to crawl forward, to breathe, get air into my lungs. My chest feels so tight, constricted. I feel tears start to prickle. This is meant to be my big day. Opening night. I've been so brave getting out there again, getting back on the stage, and now this is happening.

They will be expecting me at the theatre, in hair and make-up, to look beautiful.

The audience will be there later, all those people who have paid to see me: Jemima Eden. The blows rain down on me, forcing me to the floor. Another slap and I taste blood as my lip swells and splits. His fist on my head, thumping down… So much pain, thudding, aching, spreading. *Get up, Jemima*, I tell myself, trying to find the strength to get away from him. George's boots, cherry red, right there, by my face. He used to love me.

'Oh no you don't,' I hear as the boot swings towards me, and then the world goes black.

SIXTY-ONE

KIM

The door slammed, and I heard George shout for Jemima. He was back early. Their shared schedule had said he was due to fly in later this afternoon, plenty of time to get to the theatre for opening night. He had made a big fuss of it, had asked me to send his theatre ticket to him, so he could go straight to the theatre if there was any issue with his flight. He must have changed his ticket. I wasn't sure Jemima would be pleased. She had been so much calmer without George around, focusing entirely on the play, on her own routine. Had he heard the news? Was that why he had come back so early? He clearly wanted to be here for Jemima, to support her. And perhaps support me, too?

Right, time to get going! Mustn't forget anything. I look around the basement, taking it all in – the shabby sofa, the cramped bathroom, a pile of my old clothes on the floor. OK, script in my bag, though I knew I didn't need it. Water bottle. Mum's old blanket, as it was often cold backstage, sitting around, waiting. I could take that with me, keep her close to me. She would like that. She'd never missed one of my shows.

Above me, footsteps. The sound of Jemima getting ready.

Good. She had form for keeping me waiting, a regular reminder of who the star was here. No, the footsteps were closer than that. On the stairs, coming down to the basement? Was someone coming to get me? I was nearly ready, if so.

'Ready!' I called out. I pulled on my shoes, tied the laces and grabbed my favourite jacket from the back of the door. *Right! Opening night. Bring it on.*

But when I reached the door, it was stiff, and wouldn't open. I turned the handle again, pulled a little firmer. I hadn't locked it, had I? No, this made no sense. I tried again, pulled harder.

And then it hit me. Someone else had locked it. From the outside. I stepped back, tried to think.

Who would do this? Jemima? She knew we had to leave soon. George? No. There must be someone else in the house. I had a key somewhere, I could unlock it. My hands fumbling, I inserted the key, and tried to turn it. Something wasn't working, it felt stuck, tight. I peered into the keyhole. There must be a key in the door, on the other side.

I looked around, panicking. The window to the front of the house was tiny, but it opened a little. Too small for a person to get through, but I could shout out, and maybe someone would hear me? There were photographers out there on the street, I could call out to them. I pushed the sofa under the window and climbed up onto the back and tried to reach up to the window. *This is crazy, Kim, you aren't thinking clearly. Just phone someone!*

Jemima. I could call her, and she would come down and get me. My fingers were trembling as I called. The phone rang for a second, and then the signal cut out. *Damn.* I held the phone out towards the window and tried again.

'Hello, darling! Thank you for calling. Leave a message!'

'Jemima, where are you? I'm locked in downstairs.'

She wouldn't have gone to the theatre without me... would

she? That made no sense. I scrolled through trying to find George's phone number. I could try him next. Or the police.

And then I heard a loud thump, overhead, as if a heavy weight had hit the floor. I flinched, looked up. Low voices. Couldn't make out what was being said, but George and Jemima were definitely up there. Up above my head, in the kitchen. Could they not hear their phones? Oh god, had someone broken in?

'Hey!' I shouted, as if my voice would travel through the floors and ceiling and into the room above. I ran over to the door and tried the key again. No joy. I slammed the door with my fists in frustration. I had to get out of here. I was needed at the theatre. *This can't be happening to me...*

SIXTY-TWO

KIM

'Kim? Are you in there? Are you OK?'

George! I heard footsteps on the stairs, and then to my immense relief, the door opened. *Thank god.*

'I was locked in!' I crashed into his arms. George held me close, his arms firm around my body. I felt myself relax into him.

'I heard you banging. The door was fine. Are you OK?'

'I'm sure the door was locked, George. I couldn't open it.' Was I going crazy? And then it hit me. Jemima really must have locked me in. But why? Because she didn't want me in the play. But... everyone would wonder where I was, and we'd all rehearsed so hard, why would she do that? To ruin this for me.

'Kim, listen to me. Jemima can't go on tonight. She's in no fit state. All this press attention, it's really got to her.' George looked exhausted. He must have been up very early to get here. Had he slept at all?

George put his hand on my arm and looked at me with gentle concern. 'I'm afraid this is very like Jemima. She gets herself into these situations, becomes very unstable. She might even have locked you in, I don't know. We've been through all this before – her stage fright is debilitating. It's why she's done TV work for so long. It's been very difficult for us both.'

He watched me pick up my bag and jacket, then I followed him upstairs.

'Don't worry. I can call Elle and Vikram. Let them know.'

This made no sense. Jemima had worked so hard on the play, had put so much effort into learning her lines, and she had seemed to be calming down earlier. There was no way she would pull out, last minute...

'Where is she? Should I go and talk to her?' My mind started to spiral. Jemima had wanted to do this play so badly, and I was no threat to her. I was just the understudy.

George shook his head. 'She's gone to bed. I'm so sorry you have to experience this side of her. For some reason she must have locked you in. I don't know why. Jealousy perhaps... who knows, with Jemima. I'll try and get a doctor over to see her. Calm her down.'

I tried to process it all. What did I know? I had only known her a few months. And she was an actor, of course, good at showing people what she wanted them to see.

The door to the kitchen was shut, which was unusual.

George placed his arm around my shoulders. 'You've been so good to her, Kim. Thank you for everything you've done. But she has problems... it's incredibly sad. Don't you worry. I'll deal with everything.'

Something wasn't right here. His body felt tense, agitated. I could smell stale sweat, which was unlike him – normally he smelled amazing. I stepped back from him, tried to think.

He smiled at me. 'You really are so like her. In the early days. You look similar, of course, that red hair. And you sound like her. It's uncanny. I knew that the first time I saw you.'

Was he trying to reassure me? It felt strange, standing there, just the two of us. But some part of me had wanted this, too. To be here, with George, in this amazing house. To be close.

'OK, well... I guess I need to get going, then.'

'Of course, Kim. But first, sit with me for a second.' He took my hand and led me over to the stairs, and he pulled me down to sit beside him, a few steps up, close together, side-by-side.

I glanced upstairs. If Jemima wasn't well, then would I need to understudy for her tonight? A wave of panic flooded through me. Was I actually going to do Jemima's part? On the opening night? Surely Vikram would cancel or postpone opening night – people were coming to see Jemima, not me. This was a potential disaster for the play. I could only begin to imagine the press response, the fall-out, if Jemima didn't show up. But then, maybe it would bring more people to see the play, might help sell tickets? I had to get to the theatre and find out if I was needed tonight. *I might need to rehearse, do a run-through with the other actors.*

George was pulling me towards him. 'You OK? I lost you there for a moment.'

'Just trying to take it all in, what this means...' I replied, my voice slightly muffled against his shoulder.

'When we first met, Jemima and I, we wanted the same things. Success, of course. To prove to people that we were talented. Both of us came from nothing.' He smiled at me. 'You probably don't know that about us.'

I shook my head.

'I can see that in you. That energy and hunger. I recognise that in you.' Why was he telling me this now – some sort of pep talk, ahead of opening night? Trying to give me a boost, offer support ahead of whatever tonight might bring?

'We were the most perfect couple, Jemima and I. Everyone thought that. We were invited to all the parties, knew everyone in the business between us. We could help each other. A team. And it worked!' George was smiling at the memory. I glanced towards the door, not wanting to interrupt him, but eager not to be late.

'But you live here, you see what it's like now. Jemima can be so difficult! In many ways, you and I are better suited. We want the same things... family.' He turned to look at me, and I felt his arm slide around my waist, firmly.

'It was so lovely seeing you with my sister. And Joanna. You were so good with them. Jemima was never comfortable with my family, with children. She knew I wanted children, but it was always about *her* job, *her* career.'

I looked at him, confused. Where was he going with this?

'And I helped you, didn't I, Kim? I could see your potential. When no one else could.' George was now staring at me, focused, serious.

'I hear you, George, and I'm so thankful. But I need to go to work. To the theatre. They are expecting me.' I tried to stand up, but George's arm was tight around my body.

Somewhere in the house, a phone rang. Mine? No. My bag was right there in the hallway, just by the front door, a little out of reach, and it wasn't my ringtone anyway. The kitchen? I glanced at the kitchen door. Whose phone was ringing in the kitchen?

George reached out, and I felt his hand run over my hair, tracing the side of my face. He was so close to me, I could hear him swallow. 'That night we went to the screening. You in the green dress. It was so obvious to me! You and I... we have a special connection. I can see it so clearly now.' He sounded so sure of himself, so sure of what he was trying to tell me.

'But you're married to Jemima...'

It was just a few steps to the front door, and then I would be outside, could get some air, breathe, and think. I stood up, then felt George pulling me down, firmly, next to him.

George shook his head. 'It's over. She knew I wanted children, a family. But she only cares about her career. We lost a baby, did you know that? I thought we both wanted to try again, to do anything we could to bring a child into our lives, to live in this house. It would be paradise.'

He looked at me, willing me to understand. 'It was work that made her lose the baby. I'm convinced of it. The long hours, the pressure. It was too much for her. And now she wants that again? She doesn't care what I want...'

And then I saw it. On his sleeve. A smudge of dark red, almost brown.

'George... what's that?' I stared at him.

Irritated, he glanced down at his arm, and then pushed the sleeve up towards his elbow, making the stain disappear. But I'd seen it. And I knew what it was.

Blood. George had blood on his sleeve. And where the hell was Jemima?

With a surge of adrenaline, I stood up, grabbing the banister, twisting away from him. I tried to get to the front door, but George was fast. He caught my arm, pulling me back towards him. And then his arms were around my waist and he was lifting me, half dragging me, back towards the stairs. I grabbed at the banister, but my hand slipped, as he pushed me forwards, up the stairs. I cried out, and then his hand was over my mouth, hot and clammy.

'Calm down, Kim. You know we both want this,' he murmured, low in my ear.

His face so close to mine, I could almost taste his hot, stale breath. And then he was on top of me, my face pressed onto the stairs, the sharp edges of the stairs cutting into me. I try to twist away, but he was heavy, his whole body pressing down on me. I heard him release his belt, clumsily, pulling at his belt, then fumbling at my dress. *What the hell?*

'No!' I cried out, muffled, the carpet rough against my face.

And then I saw a shadow move above me... a shout. I felt like I was about to pass out, and then all the air left my body, as the weight of George slumped on top of me. I could hear

Jemima, that unmistakable famous voice, shouting something, though my head was throbbing and I couldn't make it out. I tried to crawl up the stairs, to get out from under George, to get some air, to get out of the way. Someone grabbed my ankle, gripping, pulling. No! George is standing over me, reaching for me.

A cry, and I turn, just in time to see George fall backwards, heavily, landing at the bottom of the stairs. And I see Jemima, reaching for the banister, trying to steady herself. Slowly, her face tilts towards me, and I can see blood, so much blood. She stares right at me.

'Get away from me,' I spit out, trying to haul myself upstairs, away from her and from George. My legs feel weak, as if all the blood has left them, and nothing seems to work properly. She locked me in the basement, right? My brain isn't working, I can't think fast enough, nothing makes sense.

'Stop!' I hear her say, somewhere behind me.

I'm on the landing, trying to think. *How do I get out of here? I'm trapped up here.* And Jemima is down there, blocking the stairs, and my exit to the outside world.

'He's not moving, Kim,' I hear her say, quietly. I take a breath and look down.

George is lying still, slumped at the bottom of the stairs. His body, so still on the hallway tiles, his arm at an impossible angle. A pool of blood starts to spread, dark black, across the beautiful blue and grey floor. Jemima just stands there, next to him, so calm, leaning against the wall.

I can see the kitchen door is wide open. She must have been in there, the whole time. But George had said she was upstairs, resting.

He lied.

'Did you lock me in downstairs?' I manage, my voice sounding weak.

Jemima looks up at me, shakes her head, and I look at the bruising on her face. Her hair, usually so smooth and beautiful, is a tangled mess. And there is so much blood. Caking her beautiful hair. Running down her cheek.

George did that to her, made her like that. And she had come to help me.

'Is he... dead?' I ask, taking a step down, towards them both.

'I don't know,' she whispers.

I look at him, lying there, his body so still. Jemima is looking at me, as if I might have the answer.

What the hell do we do now?

SIXTY-THREE

JEMIMA

A lot of what happens next is a blur. There are sounds... the surreal echo of sirens, outside the house. The front door bangs open, and people rush in, taking over. Voices talk to me, to George, then his body is lifted onto a trolley, landing with a heaviness. The cold air hits my skin. A pounding in my head, the throb of where he had struck me.

I can see Kim. Her face, terrified, looking at me to guide her, to tell her what to do. And then Kim's beside me, holding me, us holding each other. The image of George on top of her, pinning her down, swims into my head. I couldn't let that happen to her... it had happened to me, too many times.

How long was it before we decided what to do? Minutes... hours? It's hard to remember. I know Kim got me a glass of water, her hand shaking as she handed it to me. I can still feel that it stung when I held it to my lips, and tried to drink. The taste of salt in my mouth. I was confused until I realised that, of course, it was blood. I could taste my own blood.

The two of us sat on the floor in my hallway, with him lying there, taking up so much space. I was ready in case George moved. But he stayed completely still, silent.

Kim found my phone on the floor in the kitchen. There were so many missed calls. People really wanted to get hold of me that day, had wanted to know where I was. I mattered to them, the people waiting for me at the theatre, colleagues and friends wishing me luck ahead of opening night. The pool of blood was growing around George's head, spreading across the tiles, seeping into the spaces between them. I wouldn't be able to get that image out of my mind for a very long time.

'We need to get help.' Kim had said that at some point, trying to take control, be the good PA that she was. Sounds floated in and out of my mind, as if I was watching the scene on TV. Did she call for an ambulance, or did I? Someone did, as people began to appear around us, so loud, taking up so much space, and they take him away, leaving the pool of blood, now turning black. *They must be so hot in those outfits! Bright yellow jackets, all those pockets, what on earth is in them all?*

A young woman, with such lovely, clear skin, speaks to me now, asking questions. I think I get my lines right. She looks concerned for me, and someone offers to take me to the hospital, but I don't want to go.

'I need to go to the theatre. It's opening night.' I try to walk, and the woman holds me, which was so nice of her as my legs didn't seem to work very well.

'I've got her.' Kim takes my arm and then we're in my sitting room, and it's so cosy in here, with my awards, my posters, old scripts, all my favourite stories and books.

Police detectives arrive, and I know that because they are dressed very smartly. Two of them. I watch Kim talking to them, trying to explain something, and they look at me. One kneels down next to me and asks to take my photograph! I can't believe he was asking that, now of all moments. *No, I've got that wrong.* He just wants to photograph my face, from three angles, and I try to tell him that my right side is my best, and it's a joke really, but he isn't smiling. And then he takes a picture of my arm.

How did it get so bruised? All that blood on me. Is that my blood, or George's? I pass out on the sofa.

EPILOGUE

KIM

I take Jemima's hand, clasp it tightly, and we raise our arms to the sky. We bow, in unison. A wave of applause washes over me – the audience love us.

The house lights come up and I can see the audience starting to stand, a few in the stalls, and then more join them, followed by people in the circle, and then everyone is on their feet, clapping and cheering. A standing ovation on our opening night. We bow again, the whole cast in a line across the front of the stage, and then we stand tall again, looking at the smiling, whooping faces of the people in front of us. We did it! The play is a hit. Out there, I know that Marianne and Leoni, my friend and my agent, are watching, cheering me on.

In the centre of the stage, Jemima Eden is radiant, like the star that she is, bestowing her dazzling smile on her audience. I can see her face in profile, the tiny microphone taped to her cheek, the beads of sweat as the heat of the lights shines down on her. I know that under that thick foundation, the bruises have only just faded, her face is thinner, her cheekbones more pronounced than ever before. I grip her hand more tightly, and she turns to me, and a look passes between us that no one else will notice. Only we know what it has taken to get here, tonight.

We had to delay the opening night, of course. The theatre company put out a press release saying that there were technical issues, and the delay only added to the anticipation. We'd worried that it would all have a negative impact on the play, but all the press around what happened to George probably did help with ticket sales. There's even talk of extending the run.

Jemima saved me from George. I would never forget what happened that day. How George had pinned me to the stairs, the heat of his body pressed against mine. If Jemima hadn't come in, I know what he would have done next. I could still feel his hand snaking up my leg, pulling at my clothes. I never wanted that. Not like that.

I can still see his body lying there, blood spreading and pooling around him. Jemima standing over him, taking in gulps of air. Somehow, she took charge, as she always does. Told me to get her phone. I called for an ambulance. Fetched her a glass of water.

'Do as I tell you, Kim. We need to get this right.'

They all knew who she was of course, she's one of the most famous actors in the country, and I swear the young paramedic looked star-struck, could barely take it all in, looking around the house, at Jemima, before attending to George. She crumpled when they arrived, shouting for them to 'help him!'

Jemima got her lines exactly right. Word perfect. I watched her perform for them. 'It was an intruder. A man. Tall. He attacked me, and George tried to help me. Please help him.'

She fell into my arms, and I held her, as she burst into loud sobs. I lowered us onto the stairs, and we sat there, with her head buried in my neck, as I watched them attend to George, to try and stop the bleeding. There was so much blood.

I felt Jemima squeeze my hand.

And then they lifted George carefully onto a trolley, and they were leaving, taking him away from us. The front door was open, and I could see blue lights flashing in the distance.

Jemima stood up, limped over and shut the door. 'OK. Now listen. There will be police next. Lots of them. We need to get our story right.'

I looked at her. That familiar face, the star of so many amazing films and TV shows. She was the calmest I had ever seen her.

'Kim. You were in the basement. Heard noises. There was an intruder. You didn't see him. He'd left by the time you got here. You just saw me and George... saw me looking after him. That's it. That's all you need to say. Got it?' She stared at me, her eyes so focused.

'But George hit you... and he wanted to...' I couldn't even say the words *rape me*.

Jemima shook her head. 'Say all that and it goes on and on. This never leaves us. We have to get this right. Do you hear me? Do as I tell you, right?'

I nodded. I watched her stretch her arms, wincing at the pain. What had he done to her, in the kitchen?

'Will he be OK?'

Jemima exhaled. 'I don't know.'

Sirens outside, so loud, and we both turned towards the front door. Police would be here any minute, and they would want to know what happened.

I looked at Jemima in a panic. 'But there wasn't an intruder. People would have seen... The journalists outside. The security cameras outside the house?'

The house is covered in cameras. The police would look at the footage, surely, and then they would know it was just me and Jemima here. But it was self-defence, wasn't it? We hadn't done anything wrong...

Jemima was looking at the security panel by the door. 'The cameras aren't on.' She turned to look at me. 'We were all in. That's something at least. And he'd already sent the journalists away.'

A horrifying thought struck me. 'But what if he dies?' This couldn't be happening to me.

Jemima sighed, as if irritated at the suggestion. 'We stick to our story.'

I leaned against the wall. It was only a couple of months since I'd first walked into this house, into this hallway. How had it come to this? This would take over everything. I could be linked to George Eden's death forever. 'I'm not sure I can do this, Jemima.'

'Let me do the talking. Say as little as possible, Kim.'

She walked over to me, bent down next to me, and winced, clearly in pain.

'We need to be convincing. This is what we do, isn't it, Kim? Act. Well, now is the time to show me what you're capable of.'

Everyone is at the after-party tonight. I remove my stage make-up and change into a dress – I'm excited to get upstairs and see the people who have come to support me. When I messaged Marianne and Leoni to say that I was going on tonight, as the little sister, they dropped everything to be here.

'You were amazing!' Marianne sweeps me into her arms, showering me with praise, and we take a selfie in front of a poster of the play.

'Matt Hemingly, *The Stage*.' A tall man appears in front of me, holding his hand out. 'You were great!'

'Oh wow, thank you!' I wonder if he'll write about me? That would be so perfect.

Vikram comes over and pecks me on the cheek, saying 'I knew we were right about you. Thank you. You were brilliant.'

His praise means the world to me. I only had a few hours' notice that Sarah couldn't go on tonight, and that I needed to be her understudy. Excited at first, the reality hit me when I was called into wardrobe to check the costume was OK. I had only done a full run-through with the other actors once.

Jemima has been so brilliant, patiently running through my lines with me, just like I have with her, all those weeks before.

I have been so wrong about her. I remember when I first started working for Jemima, I assumed she was just some rich diva, so wrapped up in herself, but she was here for me today, going out of her way to make this moment happen for me. And it has gone so well! We were both line-perfect, and had such a great connection as the sisters. It was like we were destined to star opposite each other.

If Mum could have only been here tonight, it would have been perfect, but in a way, I have a new family now. Marianne hands me a glass of Champagne, and we toast. It wasn't her that leaked those stories about Jemima – that had been George, would you believe? Jemima told me all about it. I really regret that I thought so badly of Marianne, even for just a second. I need to work on my trust issues, get used to having friends.

Elle looked into it all for Jemima. Jemima's agent knows everyone in the business, and George had been spreading rumours about her for a while. That Jemima was unreliable. Had a drink problem. Was planning to get pregnant. George let potential directors join the dots, and they had clearly decided that Jemima Eden was not someone to trust with a big project. Elle is busy setting them all straight now, looking after one of her most talented clients.

Marianne is oblivious to all of that, and is chatting away to me about her own new project – she's working on a new TV series that's being commissioned for a second series, and she thought I'd be perfect in it. I promise to talk to Leoni about it. Working together again would be such a joy.

And then the sea of people part, and Jemima makes her entrance. She looks incredible – such poise, smiling at those she passes by. Wearing the most beautiful cream dress, clearly the star here. Seconds later, she stands in front of me, and gently taps my glass with hers.

'We did it, kid. Congratulations.'

We smile at each other. Only we know what that really means. How we had to deal with the police, and the press, and we'd held it together. Got our lines right.

Rory Jackson appears behind Jemima, and pulls her into a hug, telling her how brilliant she was. He's been round the house a few times, and I often heard laughter coming up the stairs. I've decided to stay on in the house, for at least as long as the play is on. It makes sense to be there for each other, as long as I'm needed. And, well, now I have my own room, my own floor almost, it would be crazy to move out.

I really do have it all.

JEMIMA

The reviews are outstanding. *The Stage* love it, giving the play five stars. I'm particularly pleased with this line:

Rising star Kim Conner shone in her role, showing the perfect combination of vulnerability and strength that this part needed.

Ah, Kim would love that! I should get it framed for her, so she can hang it in her room. She really is the most natural actor. And I like having Kim in the house with me. She's incredibly useful and supportive. And having her close by means that I can keep an eye on her, that we can keep our secret together.

This part of the review was lovely, too, about me:

A delicate, nuanced performance by Jemima Eden, showing that she can not only command the small screen, but can captivate any audience. She had us all in the palm of her graceful hand.

I knew I could do it! I'd shown them. George was wrong about me, undermining my confidence all that time. Trying to ruin my career.

Rory has been round a few times, and we have promised to go out more, do normal things like go for coffee and things like that, like friends do. When he's ready to come out to the world, I will be there for him.

I really must read this review to George, next time I go to visit him. I don't want to go, not really, it gives me the creeps going to that place. But I need to play the part of the dutiful wife. The hospital team tell me that he looks forward to my visits, but they don't know that for sure, as he can't say anything, lying there, far away in his own world. I think, perhaps, that its them that look forward to my visits. It adds some glamour to their dreary lives.

The police tell me that they aren't making any progress finding an intruder, and I tell them that George and I are so thankful for their efforts, and that they really can do no more. I cry and tell them that I am praying he will recover. They nod, try and soothe me, and then we all get on with our days.

I can never stay very long at the hospital anyway, as I need to be here, at the theatre each night. Exactly where I belong. On stage, in front of my audience.

A LETTER FROM THE AUTHOR

Dear reader,

Huge thanks for reading *The Other Mrs Eden*. I hope you were hooked on Kim's and Jemima's journeys. If you want to join other readers in hearing all about my new releases and bonus content, you can sign up here:

www.stormpublishing.co/becky-alexander

If you enjoyed this book and could spare a few moments to leave a review that would be hugely appreciated. Even a short review can make all the difference in encouraging a reader to discover my books for the first time. Thank you so much!

If you read my first novel, *Someone Like You*, you know that I am obsessed with actors and the acting world. Just why do they put themselves into such a competitive and cut-throat industry? Like Kim, so many people aspire to drama school, getting an agent and then making it big. Is showbusiness always as glamorous as it looks? Or are actors just better at pretending?

I am also fascinated by female friendship and its enormous impact on our lives. It's a theme that runs throughout my novels, as I believe it is female friends who truly see us. For better or worse. Please do find me on social media to share your thoughts on this!

Thanks again for being part of this amazing journey with

me and I hope you'll stay in touch – I have so many more stories and ideas to entertain you with!

Until next time,

Becky Alexander

 x.com/beckyalex_books

instagram.com/packedwithgoodthings

tiktok.com/@beckybooks88

ACKNOWLEDGEMENTS

Thank you to you, the reader, for taking a chance on this book. There are so many amazing books to read out there, and you picked this up, so thank you. I often read the acknowledgements first, so if that is you – I see you! The positive feedback and encouragement of my friends and readers kept me going through the many hours tapping away. The blogging and reviewing community have been amazing – honest and insightful. Thank you for your time and support of writers.

Thank you to Kathryn Taussig at Storm, who guided and shaped this book in so many ways. To Naomi Knox, Alexandra Holmes, Elke Desanghere and Oliver Rhodes for everything you do at Storm – what a dynamic and talented team! Thank you to my fellow Storm authors who have been generous and open with their support. We chose well. Thank you to Charlie Campbell and Sam Edenborough at Greyhound Literary for spreading the word, and getting my books out into the world.

I have been a non-fiction book editor for years, and I know how important copyediting and proofreading is to creating a good book. I would like to thank Liz Hurst and Maddy Newquist here, for your meticulous work.

A massive round of applause to Josie Charles, who read the audio version of *Someone Like You* – I am so pleased you were able to fit in this one, too. Your voice is perfect for Jemima and Kim. I know many actors listened to *Someone Like You* and loved it, and they can be a tough crowd, so well done, you!

Thank you to Nick Hern and Lucy Kirkwood for allowing

us to use a snippet from the actual script of *Mosquitoes*. I first saw a production of this by the brilliant OVO theatre company. Do see it if you can; it's a fantastic play.

Thank you to my early readers – Steve Alexander, Katie Lobina and Ally Zetterberg. I treasure and value your insight. Thank you again to my Curtis Brown course alumni for your ongoing enthusiasm and chat – you make this whole process a lot of fun.

A final thank-you to the school drama teachers out there – you bring so much to the young people you teach (and their parents). Every school should have a well-funded, thriving drama department, and every kid benefits from studying the arts. Despite what I write about, I truly think the world is a better place for having actors in it.

Printed in Great Britain
by Amazon